COWBOY PROTECTION

MERRY EVERYTHING
BOOK 2

JODI PAYNE

BA TORTUGA

This is a work of fiction. Names, characters, places, and incidents either are the product of the author's imagination or are used fictitiously. Any resemblance to actual events, locales, organizations, or persons, living or dead, is entirely coincidental and beyond the intent of either the author or the publisher.

Cowboy Protection
Copyright © 2022 by Jodi Payne & BA Tortuga

Cover illustration by AJ Corza
http://www.seeingstatic.com/
Cover content is for illustrative purposes only and any person depicted on the cover is a model.

ISBN: 978-1-951011-85-7

All rights reserved. This book is licensed to the original purchaser only. Duplication or distribution via any means is illegal and a violation of international copyright law, subject to criminal prosecution and upon conviction, fines, and/or imprisonment. No part of this book may be reproduced or transmitted in any form or by any means, electronic or mechanical, including photocopying, recording, or by any information storage and retrieval system, without the written permission of the Publisher, except where permitted by law. To request permission and all other inquiries, contact Tygerseye Publishing, LLC, www.tygerseyepublishing.com

Published by Tygerseye Publishing, LLC
November 2022
Printed in the USA

To our wives
Merry Christmas!

1

"Don't flatter yourself, cowboy! I was staring at your truck." Maverick Keyes leaned against his wheel well and grinned as Grainger and Hayden tumbled out of their shiny new Dodge, the twins all arms and legs and goofy grins. "Lord have mercy, y'all. You two have a good July break?"

"Yes, sir!" Grainger said, giving him a wide grin. "Me and Hayden are ready to work, though. Momma was fixin' to toss our happy asses out the damn door."

"She sent you some chow chow, says to say thank you for raising us, Mackey."

"Shee-it. I'm just trying to get you boys killed." He'd been worried about taking them on if he was honest, which he was, if only to himself. Twenty was a wild time, and two twenties somehow worked out to the smarts of a single eighteen. Still, him and Tommy had talked on it, and the twins were strong, fearless, and focused on the dirt, so he'd hired them. Now they had a solid team, with Fabiano there to work as an alternate. It had only taken about a year.

"Promises, promises." Jack Boers wandered up,

smacking one of the boys on the shoulder. "Lord have mercy, ain't it fixin' to come up a cloud?"

Lord love a duck, Jack was a hot bastard with his silver hair and his deep eye lines. They'd knocked boots more than once, but Jack was a horndog that needed something Mackey wasn't, so they'd decided ten some odd years ago to be the hand job type of friends. Still, he was the best buddy a man could have, and one hell of a safety man to boot.

"It's gonna pour, and my knees say it's gonna be a gullywhomper." He'd been enjoying the summer, but even in the south, September was whispering about autumn. "You seen Tommy?"

"No, sir. I seen y'all and Ollie when I unloaded the horses. That's it."

Mackey stuck his tongue out at Jack. "Grab your gear, boyos. Warm-up is in an hour. Don't be late."

The twins saluted him and ran off, spending more energy than he had in his whole self.

Mackey shook his head. "It's hell getting old."

"No shit on that, cowboy. We having steaks after the show? I'm starving."

"Yessir." First though, he needed to call Tommy and find out where the Aussie was. "You staying at the host hotel tonight?"

"Shit yes. I love casino hotels. They suit me to the ground. I'll see you in the arena, Mack-Daddy." Jack patted his butt and wandered off.

He grabbed his phone, punching the second number on his favorites, after Jack and before the twins' momma, and waited for the son of a bitch to answer.

"Oi, I'm coming. You're such a mother hen."

"Uh-huh. You're late." He always told Tommy to be somewhere an hour before he was supposed to show.

"Now, Mother. You and I both know I'm not. I'll be there. I was having a lick of fun."

"Don't." He didn't want to hear about whatever Tommy was doing or with who. That bastard just had to grin and twinkle those blue eyes and men and women alike opened their legs like they had a button. "Just come on."

"You want a cherry limeade? I'll fix you up, Mother."

Oh lord have mercy, Tommy knew how to make him happy. "Make it a big one. Extra cherries."

"For you, mate, always."

Mackey hung up the phone without saying goodbye. Sorry son of a bitch.

"Mackey, everything good?"

God, but he hated that voice. Cody Roberts was the president of the league, voted in by the cowboys running shit, and his direct line to God, from what he understood. "Right as rain."

"Don't talk about rain, buddy. It's going to pour."

"Bulls don't mind mud, and the arena's covered. We're good." Only one he stressed was Jack, and his mare Princess was sure-footed as fuck.

"Still, crowds don't like it. They want sunshine."

Shit, they wanted wrecks, cowboy butts, and at least one great ride. The fans gave no shits about the other. "Yes, sir."

"Your team all present?"

"Yes, sir. All checked in." Mostly. In theory.

"Good man. Have a good show. You ready for your TV spot?"

"Yup." Not even a bit. He'd just ramble on about how Sparkle Night always turned right and make faces at Danny behind the lens. "You putting Stock on live?"

He made sure not to smile a bit. Stockard Manning was the clown, was in contract negotiations, and was possibly the meanest motherfucker on earth. They got along like a house afire.

Stock and live TV? Not so much.

"Fuck you, Mackey." Cody did chuckle though. "Get to work, bud."

"Always working, sir."

Always. And his body knew it. Still, he had his team, new sneakers, good pain pills, and a cherry limeade on the way.

It was fixin' to be a good day.

2

Sidney Scott tapped the earpiece on his headset and shook his head. "Nothing."

"Can you hear me now?" Gus grinned at him and cracked up.

"No, *Angus*." He sighed. "I can't hear a goddamn thing. It's dead." Sid yanked the headset off and tossed it at his lead electrician with a sigh. "Is it charged?"

"I charge 'em every night, but they can be flakey. I got another, hang on."

He wasn't mad at Gus; he was just a little on edge. It was getting close to showtime, and if this took much longer he'd run late with his check-ins. Not an impressive way to start out. He'd shadowed Kent, his predecessor, for a handful of shows, but this was his first week flying solo, and Sid could feel the eyes on him from people who were still sizing him up.

Kent had been an asshole to everyone, including him. He'd never met someone who needed to retire so badly. Sid didn't have shoes to fill; he had shoes to *avoid*, a steep hill to climb, and no friggin time to do it. They were on the stretch into the Finals, and the fans were getting more demanding, the arena seats were filling up, and the cowboys were damn tired.

He was determined to have some fun though, and it was a new gig, but not his first. He felt like he had this. Plus, who didn't like to look at a cowboy?

He'd been watching the radar on his phone for the last hour. He didn't know why he bothered; anyone could see the dark cloud coming. Sid was damn good at wrangling his crew the way he did, but even he couldn't micromanage Mother Nature.

Gus held a new headset out to him. "Try this one."

Sid pulled it on and hit the power button on the transmitter. "Am I live?"

Gus grinned at him again. "There once was a man from Nantucket—"

"Whoa. Who's that? Angus? This is a family show, man."

"Family of what?"

Six or seven people laughed in his ear. He was in business. He gave Gus a thumbs up and tucked the transmitter inside the back pocket of his jeans.

Sometimes he wore a suit. Kent had worn one all the time. Every show. He'd decided it would depend on where they were and what was going on. If he was likely to end up on camera, he wore a suit. Tonight, he was more likely to end up in the mud, and it was humid as hell. He'd worn jeans, a good shirt, and a tie.

There was a lot of friendly chatter on the headset, but he cut it off by clearing his throat loudly. "Good evening, ladies and gentlemen."

"Uh-oh. Boss is on the line."

"Who's the lady?" That was Darlene on Camera five. Everyone cracked up.

"Time to work, kids. Cameras count off, please." God, he needed a strong coffee. Or a strong shot of something. And he'd promised himself a steak after the show.

"I'm a go on one."

"Two."

"Three, here."

The numbers started as the camera techs checked in, all the way up to number nine. That was Lee, down on the arena floor. Lee was pretty new too, and almost as daring as the bull riders.

"Cage?" he asked, looking at it.

He got a wave through the bars. "Sitting tight. I hate the rain."

"It's not raining indoors, Fisk." He reminded himself things could be worse. He might go home with dusty jeans. Fisk could end up with a whole face full of dirt. "Chute?"

"Check." That was Buck. Buck hated the headsets and would lose his in a minute. Buck and Kent had argued constantly about it, so Sid had decided not to. He and Buck communicated just fine either close-up or with hand signals.

Sid finished his rounds, making sure everyone else was in place with his own eyes when he could--the athletes, the bullfighters, the pyros, the flag, sound, lighting, medical, he even got a fist-bump from Buck--that had to be a good sign, right? Then he took his spot with the judges where he could see both the arena floor and the camera feeds.

"Here goes nothing, everyone. We're a go in five... four... three... two..."

3

Fuck a duck sideways, shit was fixin' to hit the fan.
Mackey met Tommy's eyes, and Tommy shook his head. The fucking world was insane, and the bulls were all on speed.

Danger Noodle came screaming out of the gate, Brian Peters on his back. The ride was solid for five seconds or so, and then the whole thing went pear-shaped. Brian went one way, and Danger Noodle went another. Problem was the bull was headed straight for one of the cameramen who was down on the floor with one of them fancy-assed cameras.

God *damn* it.

Mackey ran, managing to grab a horn and yank with one hand while he tossed the cameraman with his other, sending the camera under the bull and swinging him in between bull and fence.

"Tommy!"

"On it, Mother!" Tommy waved and caught the bull's attention, the boys standing over Brian, so he could move. It wasn't a second before Jack had the bastard bull roped, and Brian was up and moving.

He glared over at the cameraman. "Stay off the dirt if you can't stay out of the way."

The guy looked rattled as he got to his feet and shook his head sharply like he was trying to clear it. "I work on the dirt. We've all got a job to do, man. Jesus, fuck. Look at my camera." The guy limped over and started picking up the pieces.

Stockard came running out with a stretcher, making a big show of helping the camera guy lift the pieces onto it, then stood up and put his hat over his heart as the twins carried the wreckage away. They glanced at each other, and Stock winked.

"You okay, Lee? Maverick!"

Nobody he intended to talk to called him Maverick.

"That was a five-thousand-dollar camera!"

Commercial breaks were only so long, and he didn't have time for a suit. He gritted his teeth and walked away, just ignoring the man. He hadn't stepped on the fucking camera. He'd done his job.

"You come see me after the show, Maverick!"

"Stock's too fucking funny. Did you see that camera?" The twins came jogging back from stretcher duty all grins and laughter. "Noodle fucking killed it!"

"He sure as shit did, but he didn't kill the camera man or Brian. That's the important part, right?" Mackey fought to keep his shit together, really he did.

The twins caught on and sobered up fast. "Yes, sir."

Hayden pointed at the on-air clock. "Ten seconds."

Tommy bumped his shoulder. "Oi, that was good work. Lee will remember to thank you later, I guarantee it."

"Stupid shit. Someone ought to spank him."

"Roight. I'll tell Jack, hey?" Tommy grinned, wide.

Now that was funny. Probably totally within reason too.

One way or the other he was laughing his happy ass off when the commercial break was over.

The last section was bulls eight, cowboys zero, and before he knew it, the four of them were standing in a circle, arms around each other's shoulders. "Dear heavenly Father, thank you for getting us through tonight safe. Help get everyone back home and to the hotel safe too. In Jesus' name. Amen."

"Amen." They all spoke together, then they headed to the locker room.

"What are you guys doing tonight? Anybody up for slots?" Grainger hopped a couple of steps ahead of them. "Hay?"

"Yeah bro, I'm in. After food, though."

Twenty might have more energy, but it was stupid enough to gamble a week's pay away too.

"No gambling for me, mate. I'm going to turn in. I'm done."

Grainger waved Tommy off. "Mackey? You got plans?"

"Maybe. I might order a steak and a beer from room service. Or eat with Jack." He wasn't sure. Maybe he'd order porn on the pay-per-view.

"Maverick. I want a word with you."

"Oi, let a man change his knickers first, Mister Scott."

"Sidney. Sid is fine." The guy sighed. "I just need a minute. The rest of you go ahead. Great work tonight."

"It's kosher, y'all. I'll be right there." He turned around to face the suit. "Hey, man. What you need?"

"So, Lee is pretty shook up. He banged up his shoulder when you tossed him, and I don't think he'll be carrying a camera for a few days." The guy tucked his hands into his pockets. "He's in a mood, so I'm just going to say thank you for him. You have enough to do without worrying about my camera guys too."

Well hell's bells. "Just doing my job. I'm real glad he wasn't hurt. Sorry about the camera. Need to make 'em bull proof, I guess."

"Nothing and nobody is bull-proof, right? I'll take that hit. I do have a favor to ask though. Everyone's busy, and I know we pass by each other a hundred times a night and never even nod, but I'd appreciate it if you didn't walk away from me in front of your team. I'm never going to pretend I could do your job, but I have a hard enough time wearing a tie around a bunch of cowboys on adrenaline. You're a leader around here, like it or not, and they look up to you. I don't care if you give two shits about my authority, but please don't make my job harder. Deal?"

Oh, he had about thirty-seven thousand things to say about how bull fighting had been a thing before there were cameras. About how he didn't fucking have time to stroke the suit's hurt feelings when he was working. About how he honestly didn't give two shits about someone that thought of all them as a bunch of cowboys. About how they had the same boss, and how he was way harder to replace, and how his fucking name was Mackey. What came out was, "Yup."

One eyebrow shot up, and Sid's jaw set hard. "Great. Thanks," the guy said after a second's hesitation, then Sid turned and walked away, the long stride putting distance between them quickly.

Man had a nice ass -- lean and taut. Mackey approved.

He did like the visual.

Poor kid. He'd learn not to fuss until the adrenaline wore off. It took all the new guys a little bit.

Mackey jogged down to the locker room, finding it mostly empty, barring Jack.

"Thought I'd find you here. New biggie-wow riding your ass?" Jack watched him with hungry eyes, and there was no doubt he was going to get off tonight. Jack was bored, and he was willing.

"Nah. Just wanting me to be sweet on the floor."

Jack's laughter filled the empty room.

Mackey started stripping down, unwrapping his bad leg, getting the sand out of his shorts.

Jack leaned back against a wall and crossed his arms, watching him with interest. "There's something poetic about a fancy camera getting pulverized by a bull."

"Mmhmm. You could try roping one tomorrow night. The suit would be so pleased." He walked naked across the floor so he could shower off the grime. He figured it would give Jack enough of a show to keep him interested 'til they could get to the hotel.

"M-mm. I do love how you're built. Why did you give me up again? I'm pretty sure it's on you. Been so long I've forgotten."

"Because you're a horndog, and I'm a serial monogamist?"

Jack snorted. "Huh?"

"You fuck in wide circles; I fuck in a straight line."

There was that laugh again, ringing off the concrete walls. "Save me from hopeless fucking romantics. It's nonsense, Mackey."

"Maybe so." He wasn't going to argue it again. He knew Jack's views on the subject. "Don't mean you and me can't go share a meal, a bed."

He was tired, lonely, and his leg hurt.

"Sure don't." Jack hopped up and grabbed him the towel he'd left on a bench across the room. "Hurting?"

"No more than always." He had a steel rod instead of one

femur and an ankle that he was pretty damn sure didn't have a bit of bone left.

"Good. Get dressed and let me buy you a drink." Jack grabbed his ass before stepping away.

"Sounds like a plan, roper." He toweled off, then grabbed his briefs and tugged on his jeans. "You riding with me?"

"If you don't mind. We've got the same plans, right?" Jack shrugged into a jacket.

"You know it. Steak. Beer. Blowjob. Nap."

Jack grinned, hot and slow. "Good fucking plan."

4

After the show, Sid hit the men's room as soon as he could take his headset off and, by the time he got back, everything was shut down. The control booth was empty, the equipment was already stowed away, and the place was half-dark. Just that fast. *Boom*. And he was all by himself.

He'd had a dinner invitation from a couple of the guys on the management team though, and he planned to take them up on it. He was hungry, but he also figured it would be good to get to know them a little better. He found his way out, got into his rental car, and headed back to the hotel. It was a pretty sweet ride--a fancy, black SUV with all kinds of bells and whistles--and even better, the league was paying for it.

We have a table at the steakhouse and a beer with your name on it. The text from Bruce came in while he was driving, and he glanced at it but didn't answer until he got out of his car.

OMW. Do I need to change? He was still in his jeans.

No. We're casual.

Cool.

The casino was pretty big, and Sid had to ask for directions to the restaurant, but he found it and Bruce waved him in as soon as he got there.

"You made it!" Bruce stood up as he arrived and shook his hand.

"I did. They don't make it easy to find the place though." Sid shrugged.

"A couple of years with the show, and you'll know every hotel by heart."

"I guess." Was he going to still be there in a couple of years? He smiled and nodded, but Sid didn't remember the blond guy's name at all, or what he did.

"Great job not kicking Mackey's ass today." The long, slow drawl came from Brad Cambridge, the five-million-dollar man and one of the owners, sitting there at the head of the table.

Sid squinted at Brad and pulled out a chair. He wasn't sure how to answer that, so he just shrugged. "It was close there for a minute."

"Yeah. He's been around forever." There was a wealth of meaning in those words, but he wasn't sure what it all was, and he sure wasn't familiar enough with the politics here to dive into it.

"Seems like his team is pretty tight." Sid reached for a menu, but Tres Williams put a hand on it and closed it.

"Order the strip or a ribeye and a beer. He'll cover it," Tres said in a rough whisper.

He set the menu down. "Seriously?"

"He invited us." Tres picked up a beer and winked at him.

Okay then. He could handle that.

"I hear he's gonna be without his swing soon. You'd think Mackey would know better than to hire a swing whose wife was expecting." Brad shook his head. "Not too bright, those boys."

"How many concussions has he had?" Tres snorted.

Brad laughed. "I'm not keeping count."

"Concussions, two broken necks, a steel leg, an ankle that is mush." Cody looked at them all with a glare, arms over his barrel chest. "Y'all all wish you were as tough as him."

"Like you give a shit, Cody." Brad's dark eyes rolled. "You fight with him more than any of us."

"*Two* broken necks?" Sid said. Jesus Christ. Broken necks were supposed to kill you. Did lightning strike twice?

Bruce nodded at him. "First one was easy, he says. Second one was harder."

"Damn. He really is something." That was what Kent had told him. *Don't get into it with that one, there's something not right with him.*

Cody looked at him square on. "You have to be a little to do his job."

He nodded. "I sure wouldn't do it." *Hell, no.* Not in a million years.

Tres leaned back in his chair and grinned at Sid. "So, Sidney. What would you have done if Mackey had hit you today?"

He honestly didn't think Mackey was going to hit him over a busted camera. He knew Tres was baiting him. Testing him. He had no idea what he needed to say to pass. "Is that a trick question? I'm from Brooklyn, man. I can't promise I'd have been professional. Usually if I can get up, I hit back."

Okay, so that wasn't entirely truthful. He'd lived in Brooklyn for the last handful of years, but he was raised on a horse farm in East Bumblefuck, Massachusetts. His dad was a big man but a quiet one and frowned on fighting. Dad taught him never to throw the first punch, but after that? All bets were off.

"Like the boys would let that happen." Brad shot him a wicked grin. "They protect Mackey like a cult leader."

"Good." Sid shot back, not about to back off on the bravado now. "He might need it."

It was hard to keep a straight face. He didn't have a snowball's chance in Hell of standing up to a handful of bull fighters. He wasn't sure he could even stand up to one. They faced two-thousand-pound bulls three nights a week. He wasn't anywhere near that big.

Still, the guys all laughed, so he guessed he did okay.

A beer landed on the table in front of him that he didn't recall ordering, and he glanced up at Brad and got a nod. He raised the glass in thanks and took a long sip, relaxing. This was good, sitting down with these guys, figuring out how to fit in.

"If you can't throw a punch you can throw your weight around," Brad said, pretty much ending the laughter. It was telling how the table went quiet every time the man opened his mouth. "He has a contract. Kent was good at holding it over those boys' heads when he had to. You have an issue, that's how you handle it."

He shrugged and sipped his beer again to buy a second. Threats were a cop out. He could see how they might work, with Mackey having been with the show for so long, but Sid didn't think that was the way to earn someone's respect.

Maybe it wasn't about respect though. Mackey had made his feelings about Sid pretty clear earlier. He'd heard the "fuck you" in that "yup" loud and clear. Sid tried to pretend that conversation hadn't bothered him. He'd taken responsibility for Lee's mistake that night and said thank you. That was the stand-up thing to do. He really shouldn't give a rat's ass what the guy thought of him. Maverick didn't write his paycheck, right?

Sid swallowed his beer and looked at Brad. "Got it."

Except he didn't get it; it just seemed like he'd better say he did since half the table was watching him.

"Y'all leave my bullfighters alone, you understand? Cowboys voted me in, and y'all can't vote my happy ass out. Son, you have a real problem with Mackey, you come to me." Cody looked at the men, stood, and threw some bills on the table. "I don't shit where I eat. Evenin'."

"Now, Cody--" Brad started, and one eyebrow went up, the older man fastening Brad with a look.

"Don't. I got a long memory. I will pull it out and wave it around, iff'n I need to."

Damn. Talk about respect? Somewhere there was a textbook saying that was how it was done. Sid resolved right then to pull Cody aside soon and invite him out for a beer.

The table went silent again as Cody strode away, the tension thick enough to choke him. He picked up a menu to hide in, fully expecting Brad to reclaim the upper hand any second and remind him who his boss was. He'd been around long enough to hate corporate politics and he needed a poker face to pull off his "yes, sir."

"So are you liking it? On the floor, I mean." A quiet young man with a long ponytail and John Lennon glasses held out one hand. "Danny. IT. Austin."

That was so unexpected he blinked at the guy for a second before reaching for Danny's hand. "I am. Sid. I think we've spoken on the phone, right? Good to meet you. I have a lot to learn still, but so far things are going pretty smoothly." Those glasses were adorable.

"We have. If you're willing to meet sometime, I have

some ideas to integrate the cameras and the website to do some live feed streaming, that sort of thing."

Man, was it refreshing to hear someone speaking his language. Danny was also on to something. "Yeah, that sounds great. I'm totally up for that. I'll have a few days between here and Idaho. You have my email?"

"It's sort of my job to, yessir." He got a quick, teasing smile. "I'll pop you a note. I'm on the bus with the equipment, so..."

Could this kid be any cuter? He laughed and rolled his eyes. *Duh.* "You and Gus, huh? He's been fantastic."

"Me, Gus, and Sunshine, Stockard's sound guy."

"Sunshine?"

"Yep. Sunshine. Sister's Rainbow, brother's Moon -- they're triplets. Hilarious."

"You're shitting me." He laughed and put the menu down. "Are they all on the tour? Or is this just trivia?"

"Rainbow is a music professor at UNM. Moon is a producer in Nashville. All music nuts and super cool." Danny leaned in. "Little sensitive, though. Not ones to be teased. Sunshine can pout for miles."

"Sunshine. I better practice saying that a few hundred times so it doesn't come out with a grin when I meet him." There was a flurry of activity as servers arrived with plates for everyone, and a steak he hadn't ordered was set down in front of him. It looked rare, which was exactly what he liked. He glanced over at Brad again to nod his thanks, and the man nodded back but didn't smile.

He didn't hold those dark eyes for long. He looked back at Danny. "How often does he make these invitations?"

"Once a month. Like clockwork. Last Sunday of the last event of the month." Danny looked like he wanted to be anywhere but here.

"Good to know. I almost turned him down. I guess that would have been a bad call, huh? The steak looks good though." He picked up the steak knife that came on his plate and spread the herbed beurre blanc around a little. He'd have to learn to show up, eat, and keep his mouth shut. Danny seemed to have managed that all right.

"If you want after, there's an ice cream place downstairs where you can get adult milkshakes. Less classy. Less stuffy."

Oh, that sounded cool. "I don't think I've ever had an adult milkshake." He liked classy sometimes; he could dress up with the best of them. He knew how good he looked in a suit. But this kind of stuffy wasn't his scene. "Let's do it."

"Rock on. They've got ones with malted milk balls that make me stupid."

"Are you monopolizing Sid down there, Dan?" Brad asked, and Danny looked up, expression mild as cheese.

"Why, Mr. Cambridge, would I do that?" Oh, there was wickedness in this one.

Sid liked a little wicked. He wondered briefly if the kid was just flirty or actually flirting. He wasn't good at subtle; if someone was interested they had to learn to be straightforward with him. Plus, he had absolutely no gaydar, and in this crowd there was no telling anyway.

"Not to worry, Brad," he said with a grin. No way was he calling Brad "Mr. Cambridge." He didn't care if Brad thought he was a rude Yankee. He could own that. "I can multitask. Did you need me?"

"Need you? Nah, just curious about the new guy. I'd think that the league and bull riding would be--way out of your comfort zone." There was something in those dark eyes that screamed snake mean.

He picked up his fork and cut a bite of his steak, making a point of not reacting. "You're right about the league. I'm still figuring that out. But running a show is what I do. It's about the same whether it's bull riding, or the Olympics, or a football game. It's sports, crowds, an arena, and live TV. My dad is a fan of bull riding though. He can even name all the big bull fighters. I'm sure he knows who Mackey and the others are."

Dad had watched rodeo on TV once in a while when Sid was growing up. It didn't catch Sid's interest, mostly because he was a contrary kind of kid and just didn't pay attention. The tour went through New England at some point, and he planned to invite Dad when it did. Get some good seats and show him around. Maybe impress Dad for a change.

That would be a miracle.

Sid popped the bite of steak in his mouth and chewed, grinning at Brad. "Delicious."

Brad nodded his head, a half-smile on the man's face.

"You should bring him to an event, show him around." Jennifer Lawson was the person in charge of the fan club, the VIPs, and Sid had to say, he wouldn't do her job for love or money. She had to deal with fans, sponsors, VIPs, cowboys, and the rest of them -- all in a tight button down and fake eyelashes that threatened to take over her entire face. "We'd give him a good time. Fans are why we're here, after all."

"I'd like to, thanks, Jennifer. I'll find you when we get closer to the Pennsylvania shows." Dad would get a total kick out of being a VIP, hopefully Jennifer could hook him up.

He elbowed Danny. "Why do I feel like he's looking for someone to argue with?" It wasn't going to be him. Not in front of all these people, and not when he was so new on the job.

"Because you're not stupid." That wink spoke volumes. "Over ice cream."

He nodded, hearing Danny loud and clear. "Steak's good."

They ate the rest of their dinner quietly, and he finished a second beer, but he had a hollow leg and plenty of room for ice cream.

"Hey, Brad. Thank you so much for dinner. It was amazing," Sid said, standing up. He made his way around the table to shake Brad's hand, because that was polite when someone bought you dinner even if it was a business tab. Brad had consumed plenty of food and beer and was deep into a conversation so after Danny shook hands, they were able to escape pretty quickly.

"My body is going to hate me tomorrow at the gym." He stepped up next to Danny as they left the restaurant.

"I leave that gym shit to the bullfighters. I eat once a day and have a great metabolism." Danny winked at him. "Man, those steak dinners give me an acidy belly."

"Once a day? That's ridiculous." He had no problem with food. In general he liked it, and it liked him just fine. "You sure you're up for grown up shakes?"

"I have been waiting for this since I saw the schedule. I've been trying them out one a day, saving the malted milk ball one for last."

He had to laugh. This kid was too much. "Oh, that sounds good. I'm going to have that too." This wasn't Danny's first tour obviously. "How long have you been with the league?"

"Eleven years."

No way. No fucking way this kid was more than twenty-two. "Eleven--wait. What? Did you get drafted in kindergarten?"

"Oh, you're adorable. I'll keep you, I think." Danny slapped him on the back. "Seriously. Eleven seasons. I got this gig out of college."

"Ha. Nobody has ever called me adorable." Damn, he was off about eight or nine years. Danny was his age. Almost exactly. "I guess New York has aged me."

"You think? You look great; I just have a baby face on account of my total innocence and shit."

He snorted, possibly too loudly, and that made him laugh. "Innocent after eleven years around this crowd? Come on. Tell me about Brad."

"He's worth a small fortune, he's been around a while, and he likes to believe he's in control. He's on the board, but...the power's with the cowboys. They voted Cody in."

"The power's with the cowboys, but the money is with... who? The board? I liked Cody, I probably should get to know him better, but usually these gigs are about the money. What does voting Cody in mean? Onto the board?"

"He's the president. Cowboys vote him in. The board is the original fifteen cowboys who started things twenty years ago. Cody's on the board, but he's the president. He's the bullfighters' boss, the guys on the dirt."

"Ohhh. I see." He was starting to get the picture. He was in this weird space being part of corporate but working with the cowboys. And if Brad was corporate, and Cody was cowboy? He knew who he'd rather be working with. "So Brad's mostly a lot of hot air with deep pockets then, huh?"

"Mean air. And there's history between Mackey and Brad, so just know that's shitty territory."

"I figured." He'd gotten that impression. Brad seemed pretty interested in holding Mackey to his contract. Hopefully Cody had a way around that, because Sid didn't want to be the enforcer if he didn't have to. He was curious, but he wondered how nosy he should be. Sometimes it was better to have deniability. "You wanted a malt? It's on me." They'd found the shake place, and he stopped at the counter.

"I do! Thanks, man. Booze, chocolate, candy, whipped cream, and a cherry. Life, she is good." Danny waved to a couple riders sitting in the back, nodded. "Seriously, thank you. You rock."

He ordered two and paid with his debit card. He was saving some money with his travel and lodging all paid for and no rent. "Hey, you're good people. I appreciate the save after Cody left; I was waiting for Brad to light into me." He squinted toward the back of the room. "They look like they had more fun tonight than we did."

"Those guys can party. That's how you know they're the young ones, huh? They're not hurt yet. The older riders are gone by now, the bull riders are either in bed or home, and Stockard is totally gone." Danny snagged them a table against the wall where they could see who was listening. Smart man.

"Stockard hasn't said two words to me yet." He sat with Danny and took a big sip of his grown-up milkshake. It was just the right balance of sweet and alcohol. It was stronger than he'd expected too. "This tastes amazing."

Danny took a deep, deep pull on the straw and moaned, the sound cute as fuck. "Oh. Nice. Two things you need to know about Stock -- one, he's negotiating his contract since it's nearing the end of the season, and two?" Danny rolled his eyes. "Last time he was live on camera, he had a cussing meltdown like whoa."

Jesus, that was all he needed.

Stock was another one who had been around forever from what he'd been told, so "negotiating" could mean that he'd made a demand and was holding out until corporate gave him what he wanted. As the show's clown, Stock was a celebrity in the league and likely knew it. There was also the chance that the league was cleaning house—Kent had been around forever too—and maybe Stock had been made the kind of offer that had sent Kent packing. Either way it wasn't really Sid's business. His business was to keep drama like that off live TV.

"Right. Thanks for the heads up. No cameras on Stock." Sid laughed at his next idea. "I'm thinking Tommy is a bad call too."

"Aussie Aussie Aussie!" Danny's eyes sparkled at him. "He's something else. Mouth like a zombie trucker, bad attitude, but he'd give you the shirt off his back if you needed it."

"He's got Mackey's back for sure. He got between us and tried to steer him away today like Mackey was a prize-winning bull."

"He calls Mackey Mother, and they're best friends. Mackey's a sweetheart; just never bother him after an event. He's high on adrenaline, and he bites." Danny shrugged, and the look on his face went thoughtful. "He's got to hurt, man."

Never bother Mackey after an event. He could have used that advice earlier. As for hurting, he could only imagine. He'd be pretty grumpy with all of that going on too. Or pretty high on painkillers. He laughed. "After two broken necks, a steel rod, and a mushy ankle? Nah." God, his drink was good. And the guy behind the counter must have liked him because his milkshake was extra boozy.

"No shit. Doc says it's like getting hit by a truck, over and over. I can't imagine."

"I see what Cody meant about Mackey being tough as

nails." He sighed, "I don't like where I'm sitting right now. I'm not an asshole like Kent. I'm not interested in playing corporate games. But it's my job to make sure people are doing theirs. That's a bad spot to be in if you want people to respect you. I probably should have done a little more research before I accepted this gig." He could have at least tried to learn something about the riders and the bull fighters, the big corporate names…understand this dynamic a little better. Sid shook his head and grinned around his straw. "Right now I feel like I'm in danger of getting my ass kicked from all sides."

"You just need to be you, man. You know your job, you be decent, and folks will be decent to you. Kent was a jackass of mammoth proportions. Just remember that it's like any other sport -- these guys got short careers, and it's all about the adrenaline, so shit gets said. Us? We got to let it roll off like water on a duck."

He nodded slowly, thinking about all of that. Short careers, adrenaline, pain… "Let it roll off. Sounds like good advice. That'll take some work though."

"That's why they have to pay us, man."

"I might have to ask for a raise then." He glanced quickly at Danny and grinned, then looked again and totally cracked up. "Call it a bullshit bonus."

"Dude! Dude, that was good!" Danny busted out laughing, the man drawing glances and smiles. Yeah. Yeah, this was a guy that no one saw until they really looked.

That was a shame because Danny was adorable. Long eyelashes, blue eyes, and now that he looked carefully, he could see the laugh lines and little birthmark near one temple. Pretty.

Oh. Oh, he'd definitely had too much grown-up dessert. It was time he turned in before he got himself in trouble.

Sid set his cup down on the table and groaned. "Man, I'm full. And I should probably head for my room."

"You want to come to mine? I got *Fight Club* on streaming, and it's all queued up."

Did he? Yeah, he totally did. Probably wasn't a good idea, but he could be talked into a bad decision. He couldn't tell for sure what kind of invitation that was, though. He leaned in closer. "*Fight Club*. Sure. You know I'm a little drunk right?"

"Honey, I promise not to molest you. I just want to hang out, make a new friend, and enjoy this amazing buzz."

In that case—Sid picked up his cup again and sucked down the last of it until his straw made a slurping sound. He scooted it around in the bottom until he got every drop, then popped it back down on the table again. "Hey, molest away. Or friends is good too. Totally good. Whatever. I'm easy." He was. Especially when he was drunk.

"Good deal. Come on, man. Let's go hang out. Lord knows I need a friend." Danny got him up and moving, heading for the elevator.

He did too, truthfully. "I hear that. I don't know anybody on this tour. It's so weird, you know? In New York, I'm out with people a lot: dinners and movies during the week, bars and clubs on the weekends. All these nights alone in hotel rooms are boring as fuck." That was the truth. Everybody went their separate ways. Hell, the whole arena was empty by the time he'd gotten out of the men's room earlier. He was sick of having himself for company.

"I hear you. It's a bitch to be alone and always on at the same time." Oh, that was a smart way to put it, because they were always on, and the fans were always looking for a way to get to the cowboys.

"I'm sure I'll get used to it." He followed Danny into the

elevator, feeling more buzzed than drunk now that he was up and moving. "Where are you from?"

"Lubbock. Mom's a professor at Tech. You originally from New York?"

"No. I was raised in Central Mass, near Hadley. My dad is still there. He has a small horse farm." That probably meant about as much to Danny as Lubbock did to him. He knew it was Texas, but Texas was a big fucking state.

"Horses are cool. My dad's a biker and does part-time freak show work."

Biker. Cool. "Freak show?"

"Uh-huh. Like a geek. He hammers nails in strange places and frightens people. It's different." Danny dropped a wink. "Not a cowboy, huh? But different."

He'd never seen anything like what Danny was talking about. "Definitely not cowboy different." He followed Danny off the elevator and down the hall and leaned against the wall by the door while Danny dug around for a keycard.

The safety man came stumbling out of a door, shirt unbuttoned and belt unfastened. Jack Boers nodded to them both, a shit-eating grin on his face, looking like the cat that got the cream. "Evenin', fellers."

"Mister Jack." Danny waved, managing to get the door open with his other hand. "Have a good one."

"Oh honey, I did."

Sid was just buzzed enough to laugh instead of mind his own business, and he covered his grin with the back of one hand. Jack disappeared around a corner, and he leaned over to whisper to Danny. "I'd say he earned it."

"You know it." Danny closed the door behind him. "I don't know who's luckier, Jack or Mackey."

He snorted. "I guess we've both had too much to drink.

You just made it sound like Jack was with Mackey." Which was a pretty hot fantasy actually but...

"Dude. Jack is a horndog, and Mackey..." Danny shook his head, taking out his ponytail. "That man's got needs."

What? "Wait a minute. Whoa. Hold up. Is that Mackey's room he came out of just now?" He blinked at Danny. "Wait. You're bullshitting me, right? You're trying to get me in trouble."

"What fun would that be? You think we're the only queer assholes here? There's three types -- so straight they won't in the dark, willing to take a hand from a friend, and surrounded by cowboys because *damn*."

Okay, so he'd outed himself to the right guy. Lucky him. He looked at Danny and grinned wide. "Damn."

"You begin to understand, my friend." Danny managed not to crack up for about two heartbeats, then he busted out with it.

He plopped onto the couch and giggled himself silly. "Oh God. I seriously thought I'd have a chronic case of blue balls before I made it back to New York."

"There is always someone ready, willing, and able, man. You just need to watch and decide what you want, especially with the younger riders. Don't flaunt in front of the fans and leave the ones with pregnant wives alone."

"Hey. I'm not that desperate." He snorted. He wasn't out to fuck anything that came along. And he wouldn't have any idea who had a pregnant wife anyway. He watched Danny for a second and wondered if he ought to put the guy off limits too. He didn't have friends yet. He needed those more than lovers. "Now you've got me wondering about every guy I've met."

"Right? I've been around a while, so feel free to ask. I'll

tell if I know." Danny wasn't putting out 'oh fuck me now' vibes, so maybe they were on the same page.

"I will." He shook his head and reached for the remote. "Once I process this fantasy of Mackey and Jack."

"No shit on that. I'm not sure that I can process the bruises that leaves behind."

He chuckled. "Jack didn't look like it mattered one bit to him."

"Nope. I'm telling you. Mr. Boers is a legend." Danny turned crimson, cheeks burning. How fucking adorable--and telling--was that?

"A legend, huh? Are you going to kiss and tell?"

"I swear to God, man. I never...I like to go at it, but...whoa. I'm not unbreakable."

"Oh shit. He looks like a...big guy. I guess you lived. I mean, you look okay to me. Just the once or...?" Sid was a nosy asshole, but had Danny brought it up, hadn't he?

"Once. Ten years ago. It was after a bad breakup, and he promised he'd help me forget. It didn't work, but man, he sure tried." Danny leaned deeper into the cushions. "I'm not that intense, I have to admit. I like it sweet. Jack is not sweet."

"No. No, I'd guess not. And I'm guessing by the look on his face that Mackey's not either." Seriously, he had whack off fodder for days now. Sid handed the remote off to Danny. "Speaking of not sweet... *Fight Club*?"

"Hell yes. We can be Jack's aching blue balls."

They were still laughing when the movie started.

5

"Mother, it's your turn to get coffees."

Mackey groaned, looking across the room at Tommy and the boys. The hotel had sold out, so the league had crammed all four of them in the same room. Going out there was like cutting his wrists and jumping in shark infested waters. Buckle bunny infested. Whatever.

Fuck him raw. Worse? It was Halloween. Fucking Halloween.

The guys all wanted to wear old-timey rodeo clown get-ups tonight, so he was still waiting for a decision from up above. Sponsors were the real bosses.

"I'll pay you to go in my place?"

Tommy snorted and threw a pillow at him. "Mocha latte for me, caramel macchiatos for the boys. I'm paying, but you're fetching. Wear your armor."

Mackey flipped Tommy off and pulled on his loosest jeans and a huge sweatshirt. "Gimme cap?"

"There's one on the bathroom door, boss." One of the twins -- he wasn't sure which one -- answered.

"I'll be back."

"Lemon pound cake, Mother?"

"Fuck off."

A trail of laughter followed him out of the room.

The hall was quiet, but the elevator wasn't, and it stopped on every goddamn floor on the way downstairs too. On eight, the doors opened, and even though the car was full, a couple of folks shifted to let Sid Scott on. Sid looked wide awake and freshly showered. Smelled it too--hotel soap and a bold aftershave. Sid ended up right in front of him and either ignored him or didn't recognize him under the gimme cap. The man turned his back to face the elevator doors.

It worked for him. He didn't have a problem with the new suit, but he sure wasn't great at small talk, and he got to admire the tight little ass.

When the elevator doors opened everyone flooded out, jostling him, but so far leaving him be. He followed Sid all the way to the coffee shop and got into the long line right behind him.

"You think they'd know better than to make people wait for coffee." Sid said to no one in particular.

The women in line in front of Sid laughed. "Right?"

"I mean, dozens of hungover people? There could be a riot." Sid glanced his direction, smiling brightly and just being friendly, but recognized him finally. "Oh. Hey, Mackey! Good morning. I didn't recognize you." Sid stuck out a hand to shake.

"That's because I'm in disguise." He grinned and shook, winking to prove he was teasing. "How goes this fine morning?"

"Good. Great. The show went super last night." Sid's smile was reflected in hazel eyes that were warm, and more brown than green. "Your team was back up to four, huh?"

"Thank God for that." They needed all four of them, plus Jack, to keep the guys safe. Them bulls were strong and in way better shape than they were.

The line moved up a little. "I hear we're sold out tonight. Hope you're ready. Or maybe how many people are watching doesn't matter so much for what you do?"

"Doesn't make a bit of difference. I got to admit, I never see the crowds much. I'm focused on the bulls." Mackey didn't give a rat's ass about the people in the stands, except that they were safe.

"Makes sense. They're more my thing I guess." Sid nodded as the line moved again. The guy hissed and rolled his neck and one shoulder, stretching. "Overdid it at the gym yesterday."

He winced in sympathy. His shoulders were in pretty good shape this year, but God knew one of them was always in trouble. "You got you some salve?"

Sid shrugged. "I never know what to put on it."

"You want, you come up, and I'll borrow you some. I got some good stuff that Miz Vera makes us." He couldn't do without it, and he hated to see a man hurting.

"Yeah? I'll take you up on that. It's sore as hell. Who is Miss Vera?"

"*Miz* Vera is Parker Stephens' granny. You know Parker? Blond guy, Texan? He's been out for a couple of weeks with a broken wrist." Miz Vera was one of the dearest women that had ever walked the earth, and Mackey thought the world of her.

"Barely. I think Parker is the guy that got stuck in his rope like the second night after I started." Sid shook his head. "I'm trying, but some of these riders come and go so quickly."

"Parker's daddy was Scott Stephens. He was a world

champion bronc rider. That kid is born to rodeo." Wasn't the luckiest bastard alive, but he was born to rodeo.

"Tough shoes to fill." Sid stepped up to the counter and ordered. "Good morning. A large nonfat latte with an extra shot, please, and a large uh... caramel macchiato? Yeah. That was it. Thank you."

Ah. Someone had company. Good on him. Shit, Mackey had lots of company -- hairy, stinky, farting company.

"Need that extra shot. Saturdays are long." Sid paid and moved out of the way to let him order.

"Yes, sir." He nodded to the little gal. "I need a mocha latte, two caramel machi-doolies, and a drip coffee with cream and no sugar, all big. And I need a chocolate croissant and three lemon poundcakes, please, ma'am."

Sid chuckled beside him. "Feeding a small army?"

"Yessir. You seen my crew? They are ravenous beasts, and it was my turn to bring coffees."

"They work hard. I'd be ravenous too. Let me guess. You're the drip coffee and the croissant."

"You win a prize." He was. He didn't have him a big sweet tooth, and he liked dark chocolate a lot. "How'd you guess?"

"I'm brilliant." Sid smirked at him and shrugged, all shiny and freshly shaved, looking about as young as the twins for a minute. "You don't seem like much of a 'machi-doolie' type to me."

He cackled, tickled shitless. "No sir. I'm more of a caffeine my old a--backside type."

Fans. Fans were everywhere.

Sid raised an eyebrow at him and chuckled. Maybe the suits got the same talk about representing in public.

"This place is packed, huh? Does this happen a lot?"

Sid's order was up, and the guy slid the two cups to one side to wait for him.

"What? Selling out the hotel? Some. Depends on whether there are a lot of other hotels close, all that." That seemed to be how it worked anyway. He wasn't sure who was in charge of figuring shit like that out.

Two of his four coffees and all of the food landed on the counter along with a cardboard drink tray.

"Just feels tight. That was a heck of a line. I'm not used to the whole living in a hotel thing. I'm not sure how I feel about it yet."

Mackey dipped his chin in agreement as he put the coffees in their little carrier deal. He got that. His place now was still new to him, and it wasn't the smartest buy ever, being a ways from an airport, but he got back as much as he could.

The lobby was still bustling, but things went quiet between them while he waited for his other two drinks. He realized that in offering that salve he was going to have to explain to the guys bringing Sid up to the room. And it was in a state too. The twins were a disaster. He'd finally just given them a corner to throw all their shit.

He got his other two coffees, added them to the tray, and grabbed up the food. When he turned around he caught Sid's eyes on him, which made the man blink.

"You, um...all good?" Sid picked up his drinks and took a sip of one of them.

"Yessir. Come on. I'll warn you, the wonder twins are a force of nature, and Tommy might wave his willy at you, just because he's a turd that way." There. That was fair warning, and all this poor Yankee was going to get.

"Breakfast with the gang, huh?" Sid laughed. "Never a dull moment in this business, is there?"

They were quiet on the elevator, and he had to wonder if Sid was really worried about Tommy. Wouldn't that be funny as fuck? Leave it to the Aussie to fuck with the Yankee.

"I'm on a different floor," Sid said as they got off the elevator. "Your team has rooms here together, I guess?"

"Room. They overbooked. We have a room." There wasn't anyone listening, so he didn't bother to disguise the disgust in his voice. They were all the way down on the totem pole in the official employee ranking, and everyone let them know it. Hell, Stock and Jack even got their own rooms.

"What? All *four* of you?" Sid sounded pretty shocked. That was gratifying as hell. "That's bullshit."

"Yeah. All four of us." He stopped at their door and kicked. Hard. "Open up, hooligans! I got coffee and company."

Tommy opened the door, naked as a jaybird. "Who?"

"Mr. Sid. He done pulled his shoulder."

"Doing what, man? Come on in!" Tommy grabbed the bag from his fingers. "You brought brekkie! Boyos!"

Asshats. God, he loved them to death.

"Well, I—" Sid didn't have a snowball's chance in Hell of being heard.

"Lemon cake?" Grainger and Hayden snatched the bag right out of Tommy's fingers and flopped on the bed they were sharing to dole out the food. Tommy ushered Sid in, took both of his coffees and set them by the TV, and sat the man down on the end of the other bed.

"I—oh. I was... those are for... I'm really just here for some salve that Mackey has?"

"Stop molesting the man, y'all. He's fancy." He winked at Tommy and handed over the coffees. "Let me fetch it."

"Fancy? Oi. I'll pull on my reggies then Mother, no

worries." Tommy dove for a pair of underwear and tugged them on. "I'm an expert with shoulders mate. Want me to have a look?"

"A look?"

"Take your shirt off. Tommy'll fix you up. He took care of mine when I dislocated it last season. Even Doc was impressed." He heard Grainger babbling as he dug through his things.

"Oh. I think just the s—whoa. Okay. Fine."

When he looked up again, Sid was shirtless and Tommy was investigating with knowing—and professional—fingers. He tossed the salve, and Tommy snatched it out of the air.

"Y'all smash my croissant, and I will skin you both and use you as rugs in my house." The threat was idle. Both boys knew he'd just call their momma if they were shits.

"Yes sir. It's right here in the bag." Hayden held it out to him with one hand and sipped the sweet coffee he held the other.

"Oh. That's... yeah, right there. Wow." He loved the look on Sid's face. The guy was caught between amused and some kind of nirvana as Tommy found just the right spot and worked Miz Vera's salve in.

"Mother swears I got the best hands in the business," Tommy said, grinning like a big, red-headed monkey.

"I believe in giving folks their due. Better than any massager guy ever." Tommy's hands knew what they needed to know.

Sid groaned in agreement and dropped his head forward. "Oh, man."

"See that? I got what you need."

"Jesus, Tommy." Hayden snorted. "Why you gotta make everything sound dirty?"

"Because he's a horndog?" Grainger shot back.

"Nah. I'm an angel."

"God will zap you for lyin', Thomasina." Mackey snorted and shook his head. Lord have mercy, this poor city boy was going to think they were monkeys.

But Sid just laughed. "That was the least relaxing, best shoulder massage ever." The man rolled his shoulders and stretched his neck, then scootched past Tommy and pulled on his shirt. "It feels a lot better. Thank you. I have to get that coffee to Danny before it gets cold though."

"Oi, tell the nerd he owes me a beer still. I haven't forgotten." Tommy winked at Mackey, who rolled his eyes. Lord have mercy, Tommy had saved Danny from one handsy asshole, and it was free beers for life.

"Sure. I'll let him know." Mackey could tell Sid felt better; he was even standing straighter. "Thanks very much for the salve... and the peep show. Made my morning." Sid picked up his coffees, snickering.

Tommy leapt into action, suddenly all gentleman-like, opening the door for Sid. "I got the door for ya. Take it easy."

"Rest up. I'll see you guys tonight."

"G'day." Tommy watched Sid for bit, and then shut the door. "He's a hottie, isn't he?"

"He's a city boy, kid. They don't go for the rough and ready." He knew that. No question.

"Bah. Everyone goes for us. Ask the twins."

"Everyone," they said together, their voices so in sync he couldn't tell them apart.

Grainger poked Hayden in the arm. "It's a little tricky with four in a hotel room, though, man."

"Totally." Hayden nodded seriously. "You making friends with the suits now, sir?"

"The man was hurting, and he ain't done anything to us, so I'll be decent right back, yeah." He wasn't a dick. Usually.

Unless he was at the end of an event. In that case, all bets were off.

Tommy scooped up his coffee and dug through the bag for his breakfast. "Well, the strain in his shoulder is the real deal anyway. Probably over-lifted. You did him a favor, Mother. He'll be right by tomorrow."

"You did good, kid. Thanks." He found a clean chair and sat. "It's nine. I want you guys at the arena ready for warm-ups at three at the latest because we have a signing from five to six."

The twins made all kinds of noises, and Grainger shook his head. "Three? Come on, that's the whole day gone!"

"Poor lad, working for six whole hours in a day. You can jog with the rest of us. I don't need either one of you pulling a hamstring or popping a quad." Warm up was where he could get a hint of the arena's feel, the boys, everything.

Tommy didn't join in, just sipped coffee and grinned at him. "I'm not babysitting, I've got plans."

Lord. "I've got plans" could mean anything.

"So long as you're at work when I said, you can plan away. You got six hours. You can do what you need to."

"Don't forget your costume!" One of the twins hollered. "We bought a ton of candy to give away to the kiddos."

Oh, they were shits, but they were kind. Mackey approved.

"Better get to it." Tommy hopped off the bed, disappeared into the bathroom, and started the shower.

Grainger rolled over and pulled a laptop off the nightstand. "Which Halloween are we on?"

"H2O." Hayden flopped over on his belly next to his brother. They'd decided yesterday to binge the whole franchise. "You in, boss?"

He shrugged. What the hell? "Sure. I got no plans before lunch. Scootch over and give an old man some room."

"Awesome!" The boys moved right over for him, settling the laptop where he could see and arranging themselves like a couple of puppies to watch.

Lord have mercy, these two. He settled back against the headboard, telling himself he was never that young, and knowing it wasn't even a bit true.

6

Sid headed back to the hotel where one of the casino bars had a steak buffet and decided to park his butt at the bar and watch whatever they had on TV.

Part of the programming turned out to be a talking-heads recap of the show they'd just finished. He watched a little of it just to critique the camera work--to check the angles, the cutovers. See how it went. That was what he told himself anyway. If he was watching guys ride and enjoying their biceps and backsides, or watching the bullfighters be badasses, nobody needed to know.

After that it was a replay of a University of Texas game from earlier in the night. They were playing TCU at home. He got himself sides at the buffet and his made-to-order rare steak, ordered himself a beer, and settled in to watch the game.

It was boring as hell though. Dad always said watching football on TV was silly, because it sure wasn't hockey, and Sid had to agree, mostly. It was possible that he was too wound up to pay attention.

Thinking of Dad made him wince. Thanksgiving had

come and gone, with a warm wind blowing him in and an icy wind blowing him out in the form of his "haven't you found a real job yet" doctor of a brother.

He wasn't a surgeon, no, but he more than paid his bills and he loved what he did. He wasn't sure when he'd started to lose his family's respect, but--

Sid tapped the bar and ordered himself a shot to go with his beer.

"Hey, sweet girl, you want to get me a couple of beers when you get a chance?"

He glanced over at who was talking to the bartender, catching sight of James Boers, the pickup man, who tipped his hat. "Hey. Sal, right? That short for something?"

"Sid. But close enough. Short for Sidney. And you're Jack." *The* Jack. The one everyone called a 'horndog'. So pretty but from what he understood from Danny, so not his type.

"Very good. Me and Mackey are having a beer. Wanna bring your plate over? You're welcome to hang out."

"Yeah? You sure? I'd love some company; this game is slow as hell."

"Totally. It sucks hairy donkey balls being the new guy." Jack winked over at him. "Me and Mackey are just chillin' and winding down. Mackey needs a good, long time to let the event go."

That had been something important to know, and God knew he'd learned it well. Sid gave Jack a quick nod. "I've learned that. It's all good." He tossed back his shot for a little courage, then grabbed his beer and his plate.

Jack got the other beers and walked them over to the table where Mackey sat. "Look who I found, Mack!"

Bright, bright blue eyes blinked up at him. "Well, I'll be

damned. Come have a sit, stranger. How was your turkey day?"

"It's over." He took a breath and nodded to Mackey when the man nodded and winked like he understood. "Thanks. I'm a little ahead of you on dinner." He set his plate down and took a seat. "But I can vouch for the buffet. Totally worth the twenty bucks if you're hungry."

"Buffets are proof there's a God, and He loves us."

Jack rolled his eyes and grinned at Mackey's words. "You, my old friend, have a hollow leg."

"You got a point?"

"Hey, I won't be ashamed to go back for seconds, I can promise you that." Sid grinned at Mackey from behind his beer. "But I don't work it off like you guys do so I can't do it too often." That wasn't true; he hit the gym almost every day if there was one in the hotel. In his job he could literally sit on his ass all day long some days, so he needed to do something.

"When I'm not working, I'm a friggin' slug."

Jack stared at Mackey. "You liar. You don't never stop. Never. You go from work to ranch to work to ranch."

Mackey shrugged one shoulder, cheeks going a dull red.

Bright eyes and a humble blush--the bullfighter seemed more and more human and less like a gay fantasy archetype as he started to relax. Somehow that made him even more handsome. "Where's your ranch, slug?"

"I got me a spread outside Pagosa Springs, Colorado."

Huh. The show promo said Mackey was from somewhere in Texas...

"How long have you been there? You're Texan, right?" He cut a bite of his steak and chewed it slowly. He didn't want to be rude and eat before the guys got food, but it was just perfectly done, and he didn't want it to get cold.

"About four months, I guess? Maybe a little more." Mackey took a deep swig, throat working, then he put the glass down and wiped his mouth. "I had a place outside Abilene, was in the family for years."

Mackey and Jack shared an evil, wicked grin.

The look was magnetic between the two men, and he felt like Mackey was just begging him to ask more. "You want to get your dinner before I ask you what you're grinning about, or tell the story on an empty stomach?"

"Well, you see. My people were dirt farmers. A thousand acres of scrub brush. Momma and Daddy passed and left the ranch to me." Mackey leaned back, arms crossed, looking somehow like an old-timey cowboy, telling a tall tale. "So I'm working, coming back and forth, doing my thing. There's a decent ranch house, a few head of cattle, four wheelers. Even a stock pond with bass in."

Jack nodded. "Not bad fishing, either, eh Mackey?"

"Not at all." Mackey nodded, that grin just growing. "So one day, me and Jack, Tommy and... who was it, Jackie? Sky? Devon?"

"Sky."

"Sky, right. We was all out there fixin' to go fishing, and we get there? All them fish are floating belly up, something coating the water."

"Something. Shit." Jack snorted. "Wasn't something. It was everything."

That sounded pretty bad. "Gross. What was it?"

Mackey cracked up. "Oil, man. Oil. Swear to God, and the land is riddled with the shit. I sold that ugly piece of land for a goddamn fortune and bought myself a slice of heaven in the mountains. The house ain't all that yet, but the land is perfect."

"No fucking way. No way. Really?" Jesus Christ. Talk about money falling from the sky. "That's insane."

"You know it. I got a barn that you would not believe. Life is good."

The cowboys' steaks came, and both men moaned, the sound ridiculously sexual.

He chuckled because he'd done the same damn thing when his steak arrived. "So you're risking your neck as a bullfighter for... the fun of it? I mean. Why? You're obviously not in it for the paycheck."

Mackey gave him a look that screamed confusion. "If you do this job, it ain't for the money. They don't pay us enough to risk our lives."

Jack chuckled. "And the crazy sons of bitches would do it for free, wouldn't you?"

"God yes."

"Okay." That begged the natural question. "So what for then?"

Jack's eyebrow went up, and he leaned back in his chair. That question was apparently all Mackey's to answer.

"It's what we do, right? It's our...calling?" Mackey shook his head and cut another bite of steak. "I've been in rodeo since middle school, been fighting bulls since I was seventeen."

Sid had to believe the guy, but he wasn't going to pretend to understand it. Mackey basically did it... because he could? There had to be more to it than that, but he didn't know how to ask without sounding like an asshole. He understood adrenaline though, running a show as big and busy as a bull riding took more focus and energy than most people realized.

"It's quite a calling. And listen, I appreciate you explaining it to me. I'm new to western entertainment. I mean, I get the mechanics, but I was told the culture was going to take some time for me to really understand. I think that was pretty accurate." That was what happened when you showed up at the tail end of the season.

Truthfully, Sid would call it a huge understatement. If he'd learned anything it was that he needed to step back and watch more. Mouth shut, eyes open.

"Shit, yeah. We're insular as fuck, but we're basically decent assholes." Jack said that like it was…he wasn't sure, common knowledge?

"Except for Tommy," Mackey muttered.

"Yeah, our Tommy's just an ass."

"Seems like you guys are pretty tight to me. You look it when you work anyway."

"He is. He's a damn good man, one of the best bull fighters in the world, but he's a wild sumbitch." Mackey didn't seem like he was complaining. It sounded like a compliment.

"I'd imagine you guys need to blow off some steam now and then. It seems like a pretty high-risk, high stress job." Sid finished off his beer and waved the server over to ask for another. He wasn't driving; all he had to do was get on an elevator. He could settle into a nice buzz.

"Oh, us too, please ma'am." Mackey offered her a blinding smile, and she fell all over herself.

"Nice one, Mackey." Jack chuckled.

"Shut up, dickweed." Those blue eyes fastened on him. "Where were we?"

He blinked for a second, a little dazed by that smile himself. "Uh. We were… uh."

Damn.

That clear-eyed stare had him scrambled. He had to look away to think. "Uh. High stress. Your job." He was pretty full, but he cut another bite of steak just to give himself an excuse to stop stuttering.

"It can be, yeah. That's what tequila is for."

Sid laughed. "Amen to that. I just had a shot at the bar." Three beers landed on the table and the server took his plate and the empties away. "I guess it's a party now."

"Hoo-buddy." Mackey lifted his glass. "To everybody getting home safe."

"Hear hear. Cheers." He clinked his glass with each of them, but his eyes never left Mackey's. Tequila was definitely good for something.

"So, no offense meant, Sid, but how does a guy that doesn't know rodeo end up with your job?"

It was a fair question, and he wasn't offended as much as he was annoyed. Though not at Jack. Rodeo hadn't been his first choice of gigs. He'd been interviewing for a winter Olympics thing and was so sure he had it in the bag that he'd set up a sublease with Zach. When he didn't get the job, he looked around for others and he found the rodeo gig through a friend. It was sports, it was live TV, it was everything he'd been looking for just in a package he still wasn't convinced he wanted.

"Well, Jack. The people that hired me are idiots, obviously." He barely hid his grin.

"Honey, we know that. Have you met the corporate guys the board hired?"

Mackey choked a little on his beer at Jack's words.

Jesus Christ, there was no getting one up on these guys. His wide grin and the way he rubbed his forehead probably gave away a little of his embarrassment, but he could admit when he'd been beat. "Yeah, yeah. But we're a necessary evil, right? At least I'm not Kent."

"Oh Jesus fuck. He was a mean, mean bastard, man. You

act like him, we'll hogtie you." Mackey almost sounded serious.

"We didn't invite him for a drink. Ever." Jack shook his head. "Never."

"If I act like him, you can throw me under Noodle like a high-dollar camera." He winked at Mackey and sipped his beer.

"Yeah, yeah. I'm telling you, we got to get bouncy cameras, long-zoomy lenses, something." Mackey was trying to help, not be a dick, Sid could see that.

"That would be the smartest move, right?" It was a little more complicated than just a zoom, but the guy wasn't wrong. "I'm not even sure why they need a tech in there at all. Plenty of sporting events use overhead cameras on fly lines and the like. Football, soccer..."

"Well, you're the boss, honey." Mackey tilted his head. "But you'll have to find something for the on the dirt boys to do."

Sid waved that off. "We don't have a set up for lines. And I'm not interested in putting anyone out of a job."

Mackey and Jack both nodded together, like he'd done something right, like he'd passed some test.

He picked up his beer and took a slow sip, letting that little victory sit for a second. He probably should have known they were baiting him, feeling him out. But he wouldn't have said anything different if he had. He had a job to do, and it didn't require him to be a dick.

"I need this paycheck. I'm going to bet most guys do. The ones that aren't zillionaires anyway." He wasn't broke, but he wouldn't want to go too long without work.

"Yeah. Aren't none of us independently wealthy. I got to pay the taxes on my ranch and fix up my house." Mackey winked at Jack.

"Funny." Jack snorted.

"I subletted my apartment back in New York until this gig is over." He hadn't decided yet if he wanted this job for keeps. But suppose he kept it? If he was going to be traveling this much, did he even need an apartment? New York rent wasn't cheap. If he could just keep subletting it when he didn't need it, though, he'd be fine.

"So how does that work, man? Someone just lives in your place?"

"Yeah. I have a friend who was cast in a show in town, and he's renting my apartment from me while I'm gone. So Zach's got a short-term place to stay, and I'm not out the rent money. Works out great for both of us."

Jack tilted his head. "Does he sleep in your bed?"

"Well, yeah. But only because I'm not in it." That was an odd question. He laughed. "Don't worry, I changed the sheets."

"So is all your stuff in there?" Mackey asked. "Like your porn and papers and stuff?"

He caught those blue eyes. "Fuck, no. My porn is with me."

Mackey's laughter was, quite frankly, one of the wildest, most wonderful sounds he'd ever heard, low and happy, honest and sexual as fuck.

"You're all right, kid." Jack nodded slowly, then sucked down half his beer in one sip.

Shot of tequila for the win. He was feeling pretty damn good about himself right now.

He watched Mackey, and he felt like the cowboy was watching him too.

The guys were tight, and God knew Danny had been clear as crystal, but Jack played all the fields. Maybe it was just wishful thinking. Likely the beer talking. Either way, he could still take the fantasy of a tough as nails cowboy to bed with him tonight.

"You want another round, Mackey, or you done for the night?"

"Shit, I got to work tomorrow." Mackey sighed dramatically. "Hell to be a working man."

That sounded like his cue. "Don't we all." Sid picked up his beer and swallowed the last of it down, tossed some cash on the table and stood up. "I should turn in guys. Thanks for inviting me to join you; it's been fun."

"Have a good one, man." Jack signed the check, and they all stood, shaking hands.

Jack's grip was firm and friendly, and he gave the man a smile as he let go. "Goodnight."

If he kept ahold of Mackey's hand a second longer than necessary, it was completely accidental. He was pretty buzzed.

That was his story, and he was sticking to it.

"See you tomorrow." Sid gave them one more nod, and then headed for the elevators, smiling to himself. He'd been following Kent around for nearly two weeks and not once did anyone join them at the bar for a beer, let alone ask them to share a table. He was a few weeks into this, and here he was. This had to be a good sign.

7

It was the last event before the finals, and the past two nights in this arena had gone smooth as glass, so Sid hadn't been at all prepared for the text he'd gotten from Gus shortly after lunch time.

Electrical issues. Might want to get over here.

He'd thrown on clothes and hurried down there like the place was on fire, and it might as well have been. He could cover for a bad camera, a missing feed, he could work around human error. But power issues were beyond his control. They seemed, at the moment, to be beyond anyone's control. They had power in the lobby and on the concourse, power in the restrooms, there was even power outside the building. But the fucking arena was dark and had been on emergency floods all day.

"We could run the show on emergency lights if we had to, right?"

He shot a look at Gus. "Sure. But we can't let the crowds in. And we can't televise it."

"Oh."

Uh-huh. *Oh.*

Thank fuck this was night three, and everything was already set up and ready to run, or he'd be behind in set up too. As it was he had a whole crew arriving to find out they were in standby mode. That made for some cranky technicians.

And if one more person came up to him to complain, or to ask him when the power would be back, he was going to fucking lose it.

"Dude! Look at the dark!"

"You can't look at the dark, asshat."

"Can too."

"Can not."

"Too."

The sound of scuffling hit him before the sight of the bullfighting twins fighting did.

Oh for fuck's sake. Sid looked around to see if Mackey was on it. Part of him was ready to watch a brawl, even if it was between two twenty-year-old idiots.

"Check out the bullfighters?" Gus leaned around him.

"Yeah, I see them." The rest of him needed them to shut the hell up.

"This could be good."

"Yeah... not on my watch." He headed in their direction. "Hey!" He shouted, loud enough it echoed. "Knock it off before I knock your heads together myself! And don't try me, because it's been a bad fucking day."

"Grumpy!" One had the other in a headlock, and they were both grinning at him.

"Laps," Mackey snapped. "Now. Round and round."

The pair of them moaned, but they didn't argue, just took off for the shadowed arena floor. Sid nodded to Mackey. "Didn't see you there."

"No worries. This is a raft of shit. Anything I can do?"

"There isn't anything I can do. But thanks. I'd just get ready for your PR thing. I'm waiting for Cody to tell me if he's pulling the plug--so to speak--or what. I gave him the sitrep. He... wasn't pleased with it, or that my hands were tied by the power company." It was a live event though and there really was only one answer. If it was safe, the show needed to go on as planned, even without the crowds and the TV.

"Yeah. Well, we're here. Working. Running. Holler if you need anything." Mackey didn't seem worried in the least.

"Will do." Of course Mackey wasn't worried; he's already said he was all about the bulls. Well, that was nice for him. He gave the man another nod and wandered back over to Gus.

"You think he'll cancel?"

"No. I think we'll get power back." What he thought didn't matter; he had to be ready to go at go time either way. "So that's how we're playing this. You can have Danny round everyone up. I want to have a quick meeting. We'll do it... right out here in the stands. Okay?"

"Ew."

"Gus."

"Right. On it." Gus pulled out his phone.

One of the twins was doing round offs, one after another, which went wild, and he ended up slamming right into Gus. Gus went down, and his phone went flying.

"Jesus!" Sid jumped and hurried over. The tech was sitting in the dirt and rubbing his chest. "Gus?"

Gus nodded to him but didn't say anything. Just sat there squinting and rubbing his chest. Sid looked around for the bullfighting kid and stalked over, stopping right up close. "Hey! What the fuck is the matter with you?"

"Sorry, man! I zigged when I should have zagged. You cool?"

Sid looked over his shoulder at Gus who was hauling himself up and dusting his jeans off. He glared at the kid, blood pressure making his ears pound. "No! No. He's not cool. It's great that you have time on your hands to fuck around, kid, but we have a real problem here that we're dealing with, and you're not making my life any easier."

"Back the fuck off him." And there was the other one of the matching pair. "It was an accident. Shit happens."

Sid wasn't hugely tall, but he had a few inches on these assholes, and he found them, squaring his shoulders. "No, Tweedle Dum. Shit happens when you're working, and something goes haywire. *Bullshit* happens when you're fucking around and getting in people's way."

"Enough." The single word snapped through the air, freezing everyone in their tracks. Mackey stepped between them, eyes on the twins. "You two. Outside. Around the building twice. Now."

"Yes, sir." Without so much as a blink, the boys turned and went, heading for the door.

Then Mackey turned to him, blue eyes crystal clear, lips tight. "Those are my boys. You need my team disciplined, you talk to me, and I'll make that call. Period."

"I'm not going to watch something like that happen and then go looking for you before I open my mouth. You want first dibs, stick closer. Keep them out of my way. Or maybe I should just say... 'yup'?" Fuck that. Respect was a two-way fucking street.

Mackey stared right at him, then that upper lip curled. "That's your one. Stay away from my boys."

"My one?" He held that stare and returned it with one of his own. "Don't threaten me, cowboy. I don't play games." He didn't play, but with Mackey he probably wouldn't win either. Whatever, he'd dug his heels in, because now he had to hold his ground. "If you'll excuse me I have to go help Gus find the cell phone your children knocked into the stands. Oh, and get back to *work*."

Mackey never moved, never looked away, and it was Sid who had to step back and get to Gus, who'd found his phone and was staring wide-eyed at them like they were playing tennis.

"Oi! Mother, I got your drink." Tommy came jogging up, a huge Styrofoam cup in hand. "Boss says he's running the show with the big doors open. Come see how it'll work?"

"Surely do." And just like that, Mackey turned, took his cup, and headed for the back.

Tommy looked him up and down. "Impressive. Stupid, but impressive."

Sid gave him a once over and grinned. "I could say the same about you."

"Wouldn't be the first. Take care of yourself, Fancy." He got a one-fingered wave before Tommy was off.

Sid rolled his eyes. "Are you okay, Gus?"

"Dude, he looked like he was ready to--you really shouldn't get into it with him."

"Yeah, people have told me that. Thing is, I have to. He wants respect from me, then I need it from him. If you back down from an argument like that, there's no getting back what you've lost."

Gus looked horrified. "But what if he'd hit you?"

"I'm pretty sure he'd have knocked my ass out." But taking a punch was better than looking scared, even if he ended up on the floor.

"Wow. You might be worse than he is."

"Nah. That's just the Brooklyn talking. If you're good I need you to call that meeting. We have to--"

The lights came on.

There was a second of quiet and then cheering from all over the arena.

"Yes!" He'd love to celebrate but they were in show mode now. "All right, Gus. Can you--"

"Power everything back up, test the headsets, get Danny to check the camera feeds. On it." Gus leaped into action.

"Awesome." He followed Gus into the stands and went to find Buck.

8

"You okay, Mother?"

"Not now, Tom." He was in the locker room showers doing pushups. Hitting tile was hard on the wrists, and his leg hated burpees, so he pushed up.

Motherfucker. Challenging his ass. The twins were full of piss and vinegar, sure, but Grainger had apologized, and it had been an accident. Not only that?

You didn't rag on his team. He was head of the best bullfighters in the motherfucking world, and he knew it. No pansy-assed asshole got to push him.

"You're going to overdo it." Tommy leaned in the doorway and crossed his arms. "Forget that guy."

"I'm trying. Fuck, man. The kids were ramped, sure, but it was a stupid fucking accident, nothing intentional."

"This is new. Never seen you crack the shits over a suit, mate. Then again, I've never seen a suit make a decent go at you either." Tommy sounded amused.

"Can you believe the little fuck? Snarling at me?" He stared at Tommy. "When I have been nothing but decent. Every fucking time. No more. Let the bastard hurt."

Tommy shrugged. "Imagine what Cambridge had to say about this? Sid probably got an earful and then some. Tech without power is kinda the definition of a bad day."

"Sucks to be them." Not now. He was pissed. He'd get unpissed; he knew that about himself, but he wasn't ready. Not yet.

He needed a chance to breathe before he could screw his head on straight, and if he didn't get that? Fuck a doodle goddamn do.

"Roight. Fuck 'em." Tommy jumped right on board. "We don't need their fancy cameras to do our job. Bulls don't give a shit how they look on TV."

"No. No, they most certainly do not. Shit, we're here for the cowboys, full stop. The rest ain't for us."

"That's right. And those boys might be knuckleheads off the dirt but they're damn reliable when it counts, hey?"

"You remember being twenty?" He did. The list of shit he'd pulled could fill about thirty notebooks -- just from that year.

"Mostly." Tommy gave him a wide grin. "I might have been a tad impaired. I was a right wanka."

"Was. Right on. I was a devil and a half." Nothing serious, mostly pranks, but still, more than the twins had done.

"The kids watch themselves because they think you'll report to their momma." Tommy didn't ask if he was done, just stepped into the showers and held a hand down to help him up.

He let himself be hauled. "They're good boys, and damn good at the work. I like them both." They were young, dumb, and full of come, but decent at the soul level.

"Good thing or you'd've let 'em get trampled by now."

"You ever been 'round the outside of this place, boss? It's fucking *hugemongous*." Right on cue the twins arrived, pink cheeked and still slightly out of breath.

"Well, you ran out that bonus energy, didn't you?" Buttheads.

Grainger flopped on the bench like a soggy puppy. "Yessir."

"Anybody got water?" Hayden joined his brother, leaning up against the wall.

Tommy just shook his head. "Almost time for that autograph thing, Mother."

He tossed over two waters. "Clean up and get your asses upstairs. I'll cover for you until you show. Fair?"

The boys caught the bottles easily. "Yes, sir." Hayden got to his feet and pulled Grainger up with him. "We clean up fast."

"You got a smile yet?" Tommy elbowed him, teasing as they left the locker room. "You're pretty when you smile."

"Butthead." Lord have mercy, no one could soothe him like Tommy. No one on earth. "I'm pretty whenever I'm standing next to your scary ass."

That made Tommy cackle. "Only because you got more teeth."

They leaned together a second, howling with laughter, which was of course when the city boy and his crew walked by.

"They're having fun today, huh?" Gus shook his head as they walked by.

Sid glanced over with a flash of heat in his hazel eyes. "Glad someone is."

He looked at Tommy, who looked right back and winked. In unison they gave the two-fingered salute.

"Aussie Aussie Aussie!" He muttered, and Tommy answered.

"Oi oi oi!"

9

Another weekend, another arena.

Oklahoma, Indiana, Utah, Wyoming, California... he wasn't even sure where he was right now.

Sid grinned at himself. That was bullshit, and he knew it. This was the week of the league finals, he was in Vegas, this was a big damn deal, and everyone was riding his ass.

He was feeling ready for a break. Maybe he'd go somewhere amazing between now and late January. It didn't have to be New York; it could be anywhere, just somewhere that had a view of something besides a parking lot and something to do that wasn't streaming on his laptop. He sure wasn't going home. Thanksgiving had been enough for one holiday season.

Yeah, a break sounded good, but even so, he had to admit he was starting to like this rodeo gig. He was getting the hang of this thing. He didn't miss the anxiety he'd felt in the beginning, getting through the first few arenas, but he'd gotten the way of loading in and loading out. He knew a lot more names and faces, and he'd even earned cred with his crew. Best of all he wasn't worried about fucking something up anymore. He still made some mistakes now and then, but only small ones, and he usually knew how to fix them.

He was starting to get into the rhythm of the show too. He understood the mechanics of the sport better, and he'd begun to anticipate sometimes—learning the silences and the tension and the parts of the show where the crowd would go nuts.

All of that made his job easier. He knew what to focus on and what not to, what the crowds wanted to see up on the big jumbotrons, and what they didn't.

But that also meant he could tell when the energy was off. When something wasn't connecting.

It was the second weekend here in Vegas, and the crowd was excited. But overall, the show just hadn't settled down yet, and something was especially off with the bull fighters. Everything seemed to be a little out of sync, and that wasn't right, it wasn't like them.

He had to wonder if Mackey had fought with the twins or something. That team was usually tighter than a nun's thighs.

Honestly, though, he couldn't see those two fighting with Mackey. They worshipped him. Maybe Tommy was hung over or something. Whatever it was it looked like work out there tonight. Even the bulls were extra-ornery.

"Stand by. We're going to cut to commercial after this ride. Gus, I'll want Stock up on the big screen. Let's stay off the bull fighters this break. Number two you can pick up Jack."

He barely registered the chorus of "standing-by," he knew. He watched the cowboy in the chute getting settled and tugging on his rope. He could tell by the vest it was

Reed Hunt. Reed was having a tough season; he'd started out injured, and that hadn't gotten any better for sure.

The bull wouldn't stop leaning on the gate, so Tommy climbed up with a two by four, shoving at the bull to encourage him to stand up.

Mackey frowned, the bullfighter dancing, hopping from one foot to another, tension written on the man's body.

"Gus, what bull did he pull? Do you have the lineup?" He'd put money on Tuff Nut. The leaning thing had been happening a lot with him. Maybe not so much leaning as fighting to get out. "There's a lot going on in that chute."

"Uhn...Tuff Nut? He's a grumpy old bastard."

"Right? I--"

The gate flew open with Tommy still on it, slamming hard enough to send the Aussie into the next gate behind and crumpling to the dirt.

Reed was fouled out of the gate and headed into the well, the bull spinning him down. The bull fighters were right there, and when Reed's hand popped out of the bull rope, Sid waited for the bull rider to hit the ground.

But that didn't happen.

Well, Reed's head and shoulders hit the ground, but the man's spurs were caught in his bull rope and the bull took off across the arena floor, the bull fighters and Jack following.

"Holy fuck. Two, pick up Tommy and stay on him. Five... on the bull. Three and six, show me the crowd but stay the hell off the family area okay?" He didn't know if Reed had anyone here, but if so, they didn't need to be on camera for this.

Sid glanced at Tommy just long enough to see the man getting helped up, then he turned his attention back to the bull.

In those few moments, Mackey had launched himself onto the back of Tuff Nut, knife in hand, and was sawing at the rope as one of the twins grabbed Reed and wrapped around the kid's head.

"Jesus, you see that?" Gus shouted.

Yeah, he saw it. Mackey was *on* the fucking bull.

It seemed to take forever before the rope was sawed through and broken, Reed and Mackey both crashing to the ground, but it was only seconds.

Seconds.

"One, find Buck, bring Shane to interview him after this nightmare is over." For something like this he liked to get the Arena Director's take before cutting to the cowboys.

Tuff Nut whirled around, and Jack threw a loop, but missed, and he heard Mackey snap out, "Hey!"

It was loud. Loud enough to make him jump, and it was made louder by the stunned silence in the arena.

The twins were on Reed now, both of them surrounding him, and Mackey grabbed Tuff Nut's horn, pulling hard. "I said hey!"

The bull turned on Mackey, so fast Sid's eyes could barely track it, and there was a look of fury and satisfaction on Mackey's face.

The blow came hard and fast, sending Mackey through the air, and when Tuff Nut came for round two, Mackey was back on his feet. All by himself.

The second run had way more power behind it, but Jack roped the bull and tugged, spinning Tuff Nut away right before they collided.

Sid barked out another round of orders to his cameras, heart pounding. Mackey was either the bravest man on earth or he was a complete lunatic. Didn't really matter, either way he'd kept that bull from killing Reed, without much regard for whether Tuff Nut decided to kill him instead.

There was a flurry of horses and cowboys as Jack forced Tuff Nut off the dirt. That was always cool to watch, but all Sid could do was stare at Mackey. The bull fighter was pumped up, the adrenaline seemed to make him glow.

Tommy ran up, stopping next to Mackey for a quick word before jogging over to the twins.

Sports medicine was all over Reed, and Mackey went to the kid, kneeling down to put one hand on Reed's shoulder, all four of the bull fighters praying for him. It didn't matter if it worked, because damn, it was a powerful, moving sight.

Sid found himself nodding and whispering, "Amen."

And then he had to get back to work. "Two, let Tommy go and follow the stretcher. Everyone stand by for commercial in five, four, three, and... cut. One, you got Buck?"

"Yes, sir."

"Sid," That was Lee in the arena. "I've got the bullfighters close you want me to--"

"No. Let's leave them alone." They were hurting, and that was terrifying. It wasn't their night. It wasn't anybody's night.

"Right. Gotcha. This is going to be a long one, huh?"

"Yeah." Jesus Christ. They still had half the night to go, and all of them were moving stiffly. Tommy was his getting ribs taped. It looked like Mackey had refused the medic, but he had to be hurting like hell.

Mackey was talking to the boys, hard and fast -- he wasn't sure whether it was a half-time chewing out or a pep talk or what, but the bullfighters were listening.

"Put up the replay." He really didn't want to, but he knew the crowd wanted to see it. The jumbotrons switched from sponsor ads to the worst thirty seconds he'd been witness to yet on the tour. And everyone watched. Everyone. Including him.

It was just as horrible the second time around. Maybe worse because the IT wizards had formatted some of it in slow-mo. And he would start off the cut-back from commercial with the same replay too. It was what Brad called "good TV."

"God, Mackey is insane." Gus's voice was awed and quiet.

Sid nodded. What was it Cody said? "You have to be a little to do his job."

He took a deep breath, shaking off the last few minutes. Mackey and his crew couldn't afford to be off their game, and neither could he. "Okay, everyone. One last good thought for Reed and then we have to let that go, we have a show to finish."

He was encouraged by the round of, "Yes, sir."

Sid glanced over to where Mackey and Tommy were standing, talking to Jack, and then they fist-bumped, three huge, scarred hands meeting. Sid had to wonder if they knew how fucking hot that was.

Seriously. Between that and the look in Mackey's eyes when Tuff Nut made a run at him--like a challenge...like a *dare*-- Sid was going to have plenty to dream about tonight.

He was probably going to go to hell for thinking someone was hot while a man's life was in danger, but at least he'd do it honestly. Then again, this was bull riding. When wasn't someone's life in danger?

As planned, after the commercial break the replay went up on the jumbos again. Sid didn't watch this time; his eyes were on the bull fighters. Especially the twins, the pair of them standing still as stones.

Mackey came over to them and shook one by the arm, lifting his chin and smiling, and then, shit, he wasn't sure what Mackey said, but those boys lit up, puffed up and stood a little prouder. It was something to see.

10

"I'm sorry, boss," Hayden muttered, and Mackey shook his head.

"What the hell for? Y'all did your jobs. Reed's hurt, but that bull – he's bad news. You rocked it. Cover the cowboy." Mackey wasn't worried one bit. Hurt? Yeah. Worried? Fuck that. "I'm proud. Let's keep it up. I need y'all to cover Tommy, though. He's staying, but no more hits for him. Deal?"

Mackey wasn't sure what the twins had fought about – could be a girl, could be a boy. Hell, it could be that one of them had used all the shampoo. They were brothers, and brothers tied it up. One way or the other, the vibe in this fucking arena was bad news, so he needed everyone on it.

"Deal." Grainger grabbed his brother by the back of the neck and gave Hayden a shake, and Hayden's face changed completely.

"We've got him, boss. No hits for the Aussie." The brothers bumped shoulders and jogged toward the chutes looking a foot taller and ready to roll.

There. Better. They could beat the shit out of each other

after the show. Although these two tended to pout and then let it go. Not big fighters – tough as nails when they waded in, but they rarely started shit.

"I hate this arena," Jack said, hand falling on his shoulder.

"Yeah, it's small. Not enough room to spit." He looked up and nodded. "Someone's fixin' to get hurt bad."

"And you're there to stop it."

"From your skanky mouth to God's blessed ears, cowboy."

"And good thing too." Jack pointed at the chute, laughing, and hauled himself back up onto Princess.

Goddamn it. Parker Stephens was up. The kid could ride, but he was running hot and cold this season and the last couple rides had been downright chilly. Parker and Reed were buddies though and Mackey liked the set of Parker's jaw. The cowboy looked somewhere between pissed off and damn determined as he slammed his fingers flat.

He took point, while the twins flanked Tommy. His ribs were creaking, but no more than he'd had before, and his ankle was holding, so he was ready.

The big Brahma jumped out as soon as the gate was pulled, and Parker rode it, bearing down with all he had.

"Come on, Park! You got this!"

The bull spun left, kicking his heels and making it look good. Parker rode like he was fighting for his life, and when that goddamn buzzer went off, Parker went down, and they moved in.

"Hey!"

"Look here!"

"No. No, over here!"

The bull twisted around a couple times, then he headed for the out, trotting like he knew his job.

He heard the crowd screaming, the confetti cannons going off, and that was good.

What was not good was the bull standing up in the next chute with little Will Nash on his back, one of the new boys struggling to hold the kid's vest and not let him fall in.

"Pull the goddamn gate!" There was no fucking good here. "Pull it now!"

The gate flew open, the bull came screaming out, and Will went down. Jack wheeled around, throwing a loop, and it caught on the bulls horns, but right behind Tommy's back. Mackey threw himself at Tommy, knocking Tom down and taking that fucking taut rope right in the chin, bouncing off his jawbone.

He somersaulted through the air, and just before he hit the ground and the lights went out, he thought, *that's gonna leave a mark*.

11

Sid sat along the edge of the arena, long after the crew had gone home, long after the ring was empty, long after the lights had gone out and there wasn't a whole lot to see by.

He'd remembered that the first night he shadowed Kent around, he'd spent an awful lot of time thinking why do the bull riders do this? He was sure that culturally, somehow, it made perfect sense to someone, but to a guy like him? Right now, sitting here and staring at the empty, quiet arena floor, he wondered why anyone did it.

Those bull fighters had taken a beating and then some tonight. Mackie had tried to explain it, but it didn't matter. He still couldn't quite get his head around the *why*. Who the hell woke up one day and decided they were going to throw themselves in front of a bull for a living? These guys were the hardest-working and hardest-hit men alive.

The twins were beat up, but the word on them was they'd be okay for Friday's show. The rumors about Tommy were slightly less optimistic. Sid was hearing that one of

Tommy's bruised ribs was now fractured at least, or that he'd broken three… depending on whose story you believed.

There weren't any rumors about Mackey. Like, none. No one was talking. Probably because no one knew even a little bit yet, and no one was going to speculate. But Sid knew bad news was possible. The guy had already had too many concussions, another knock-out might not be bad, but it wasn't good either.

"What are you doing, Mackey? They let you out of the hospital?" He wasn't sure who that was talking, but his ears sure perked up.

"Didn't go. No one thinks I'm purty, so Doc sewed me up. I lost my granddaddy's ring in the dirt. I need to find it." Mackey came staggering out, stumbling a little, using his phone as a flashlight.

"Hey, Mackey. Hang on. I'll get the working lights for you." Sid stood up. "It'll just be a minute."

Mackey turned to look at him, the motion slow and deliberate, and shit. Mackey's face was one huge, swollen, bloody bruise. "Thank you. That would be most welcome."

He didn't stare, because that would be rude, but he wanted to. Instead he climbed over a set of seats and followed the stairs up to the booth. He hit the big switch for the working lights and the arena floor lit up. That was going to be bright. Hopefully Mackey could deal.

Mackey was walking through the dirt. They wouldn't grade it for tomorrow's short go until the morning. The bull rider that had been talking to him turned out to be Parker Stephens, the guy who had been on the ride just before Mackey got that rope in the face, the man searching alongside the bullfighter.

"Gold or silver? Tell me what I'm looking for Mackey, I'll

find it. You should get off your feet." Parker's eyes were on the dirt, and he was sticking close to the bull fighter.

"Gold ring on a chain. Real simple."

"Got it. Go sit, man. Get some ice."

A ring on a chain sounded important. After a day like he'd had, for Mackey to lose that too would just add insult to injury. Sid had time on his hands, so he could help. He made his way down to the arena floor.

"You need a hand, guys?"

Parker looked up sharply. "Oh. Hey, Mister Scott. Thanks for the light, man."

Sid nodded. "You're welcome." He didn't wait for an invitation; he just took up a spot on Mackey's other side and started looking. He didn't need to see the look Parker gave Mackey; he could feel the curiosity even from a few feet away.

He didn't say anything though. He just walked and looked.

Mackey was muttering. "Gotta find it. I always wear it. Always."

"You're Brass, right Mister Scott? Can't you tell him to go get some ice and sit down?" Parker sounded worried.

Sid laughed. "I can't tell him anything, trust me." Even if he could, he wasn't going to tell Mackey not to look for something so important. He took out his phone and shined it on the dirt. "We'll find it."

"We got to. I need it." Mackey stumbled forward, but he never fell, never lost his balance.

"Hm." Sid turned the light off a second, found Danny's number and texted him.

Do you have plans tonight? Do you think you could round up a bunch of guys... a lot of guys and get back to the arena fast? Mackey lost his necklace in the dirt.

His Granddaddy's ring? We'll be right there. Simple as that.

That was exactly the reaction he was hoping for. He didn't tell Mackey; he just turned his light back on and got back to looking. The arena might be small for bull riding, but it was plenty large to lose a ring in, and they'd be there all night without help.

"That was a nice ride tonight, Parker."

"It was. I needed one." Parker gave him a worried look over Mackey's shoulders. "How you feeling, Mackey?"

"Like I tried to give a strand of barbed wire a blowjob, kid."

Sid snorted and tried not to laugh, but that was hopeless. "That'd be some lucky barbed wire."

Really, Sidney? You said that out loud? Beautiful.

"You know it, sweetheart. I've brought men to their knees."

"Careful, Mackey!" Parker hissed, and Mackey snorted.

"Shee-it. He's hanging with wee Danny. He's getting his."

Sid blinked. "Wait. I'm not... I mean, I *am*... but I'm not... with Danny. With Danny? Are you serious?"

Mackey chuckled softly. "He's a little sweet for me, but he's a good boy."

Danny would definitely be too sweet for someone who got their rocks off with Jack Boers. *That* he was not going to say out loud; it was none of his damn business. "He's much too sweet for me, but he's been a good friend. Me and Danny. Heh. No."

Mackey groaned softly, and a drop of blood splashed on the dirt.

"Parker." Sid moved quickly and he and Parker caught Mackey under each arm. "Time to sit, big guy."

"Sit? He's gonna pass the fuck out, man."

"Maybe. If so, I'd rather he be sitting when he did it."

Parker did what he was told, and they set Mackey up in a seat in the stands.

"Is Doc still here?"

Parker shrugged at him, looking panicked. "I don't know."

"Parker. Find Doc." Small words. Maybe the kid would understand small words.

"On it."

Mackey stared at him, and he wasn't sure both eyes were seeing the same thing. "I got to find that ring. My gran gave it to me when I graduated. I can't lose it. I ain't never lost it."

"We'll find it. I--" He was about to confess that he'd texted Danny when his friend came hurrying in with a dozen cowboys and what looked like their entire crew. "I got us some help."

"Don't worry, Boss." Grainger jogged up and patted Mackey's knee. "We got this. Ooh. You look bad, Boss."

"We got it if you'd get out of the way already." Hayden gave Grainger a shove and the two of them stumbled together into the arena.

"Ow. Shut up and get to work pinhead."

Sid laughed. "Some help might be more... helpful than others."

"They're just boys. Ain't even old 'nough to drink." When Mackey said 'drink' it came out 'drank'.

"Their hearts are in the right place." Where the hell was Parker? Mackey looked like shit. "Can you see down there? The place is swarming. I bet they find your ring fast."

"Thank you. I need it."

"Goddamn it! Maverick Keyes! I am going to kick your sorry ass!" Doc came running, the old man's face like a thundercloud. "You said you were heading for the hospital, you bastard! Call 911, Sid. Tell them head injury and possibly internal issues."

Jesus Christ. "That's not what he told us. Parker, go to the back and wait for the ambulance to let them in." Sid dialed 911 as Parker ran off. "Sorry, Doc."

He calmly talked to the emergency dispatcher and gave her all the info she requested.

"Not your fault, kid. Mackey's the most hard-headed piece of shit on earth. You hear me, Mack? You're a fucker." Doc was obviously trying to keep Mackey awake, focused.

"I--Doc?"

"Yeah, Mackey." The old man's voice dropped. "The bus is coming. Just hold on, buddy."

Kent had said it was best to stay out of cowboy business, like when they were hurt, that they'd take care of their own. Looking at Mackey right now, Sid decided that was bullshit, and this was the last time he was going to ignore it. If he thought someone needed help, he was going to make sure they got it. Cowboy or otherwise.

"They're coming." He was still on the line with dispatch. The arena wasn't right in town or close to a hospital, so it would take some time, but an ambulance was coming. If the guys didn't find the ring before then, he'd deliver it to the hospital himself.

Sid looked at Doc. "What's the word on Reed?"

"He's solid. Sprained riding hand, concussion. Hate this arena."

Sid sighed. He'd heard talk about it being too small both in the public and private spaces. "And we've got a whole weekend here still."

He had questions, none of which he wanted to ask in front of Mackey. How long would Doc let Mackey keep this up was a good one. He had eyes, he could see what Mackey was after.

They sat with Mackey, and Doc talked and talked, keeping the cowboy as coherent as he could until the paramedics arrived. Sid got out of the way and stood with the twins watching. Everyone in the arena froze as Mackey was carried off on a stretcher in a neck brace with Doc in tow.

"My ring, Sid. I need it." Mackey's eyes burned at him.

"I'll find it. I swear."

"Damn, Sam." Hayden whispered.

"Why don't you boys go find Tommy and get your swing on deck for tomorrow."

Grainger shook his head. "Boss doesn't miss a show."

"Just in case. Go talk to Tommy."

"Boss will be here. What about his ring?"

"I'm staying until we find it." Sid was about to go join the search, in fact. "And then I'll bring it to him."

Hayden looked at Grainger, Grainger stared back at him, and the two of them shook their heads. "I'll call him. We have to keep looking." Hayden didn't leave room for him to argue, the boys just stomped off.

Sid had to grin. They knew Mackey better than he did, right? He followed them down to the dirt.

It took the better part of an hour before he saw it, pushed up against the cage in the center of the arena, a tiny glint in a sea of brown sand. He bent down and picked up the necklace with a simple gold band on it.

He turned it over in his fingers. The clasp was broken but the chain was still through the ring. "I got it," he said to no one, kind of awed that it was found at all, let alone that it was in his hand. If everyone including Danny knew it was important, then this was a hell of a find. He said it louder, holding it up in the air in his fist. "I got it!"

A wild cheer went up, all of them taking this chance to celebrate together after a day of pure shit.

Danny ran over all smiles. "You got it? Let me see."

Sid opened his fist and showed it to Danny. "You think it got trampled? It looks okay."

"Looks fine. Can you run it to the hospital so he has it?" Danny bounced. "That'll make his day."

"Yeah, I was going to." He was getting all kinds of slaps on the back from guys as they left the arena, and he was trying to say thank you to every one of them too. The twins stopped next to him, and Hayden shook his hand.

"Nice work, Mister Scott."

He nodded. "Thanks for your help, guys. You two want to run this over, or do you mind if I do?"

Grainger sighed. "Tommy ain't answered Hayden's texts. He's probl'y fine, sleeping I bet, but we'd best look in on him."

Hayden nodded. "We got to pow- wow, and he needs to know the boss is at the hospital. He'll want to go."

"I'm gonna run over there now, then. Thanks again guys. Danny, thank you so much."

"You're welcome. I just said the ring was missing, and people rallied." Danny dangled his keys. "You need a ride back to the hotel, boys? I got you."

Sid pulled out his phone as he hurried toward the exit, pulling up directions. He'd gotten Doc's number while they were waiting for the ambo, and he texted as he got into his truck.

OMW with his ring.

Good deal. Ask for me at the ER.

He'd seen beat up. He'd wrecked a car. He knew a little

about injuries, but in his world people did things like rest and heal. They took a day off when they needed one. Mackey's version of injured was some other level of tolerance entirely.

Boss doesn't miss a show.

Sid was worried, which was an odd feeling considering they'd gone toe to toe a couple of times. He knew this ring was important to Mackey though, and whatever else was going on, the bull fighter was human, and Sid knew he was doing the right thing.

It was a bit of a drive, but GPS was reliable, and he pulled into the well-lit and busy ER parking lot in about twenty minutes. He asked for Dr. Anderson as soon as he arrived, and it only took about ten minutes for Doc to appear.

"Good job. Come on. You can give it to him. He's a little loopy and in restraints, so don't be surprised. He's going to ask you to take them off. Don't. He's got to let us do our jobs."

"Restraints? God." He had no intention of taking restraints off a 'loopy' bull fighter. No way in hell.

"Yeah. That's about right. He's not happy, but he's stressing the ring." Doc led him into the room, where Mackey was tied down, the man looking weirdly like Frankenstein's monster, a little less green, but not so good.

"Hey, Mackey." Sid took the chain by the busted clasp and hung it in front of Mackey. "I'm here. I found your ring. Can you believe that? All those guys in the arena and I found it."

"Oh." Mackey relaxed -- so suddenly and so hard that Sid *saw* it as the man melted into the sheets. "Oh, thank God. Thank you, honey. You-you just don't know what all this means."

God, that was amazing. All the tension against the restraints was gone, just like that. Even Mackey's face had relaxed. It was like looking at a different man. "No, I don't. But I'm interested if you want to tell me." Sid touched Mackey's fingers carefully. "I'm going to let you hold it okay? Will that help?"

He slipped it in Mackey's hand, and the bright blue eyes closed. "This was my granddaddy's. He died when I was a senior in high school. My gran gave it to me when I graduated, said he wanted me to remember him, how much they loved me. Said he was my guardian angel. Always wear it. Always. He was a good man. Proud of me."

Guardian angel. That explained a lot. "No wonder you need that ring. You need all the guarding you can get. Was he a bull fighter too?"

"He was a roper. Had five fingers -- three on one hand and two on the other. I used to watch him smoke and think he was pure magic." Tears slid down Mackey's face.

So this insanity ran in the family. He knew that feeling though; his own grandfather was his hero too. He swallowed and took Mackey's free hand. It was reflexive; he didn't think that move through at all. The tears were real. He knew that, and he was sure he only saw them because of the meds Mackey was on, but the cowboy seemed lonely.

"Been a bad day, honey. Can you tell them to take the straps off? I got to get some rest before tomorrow."

And there it was. He chuckled softly. "I can't tell them anything. You can rest though; you've got your ring. You want me to keep it safe?"

"I'll need it tomorrow. You'll bring it? Did you find the chain?"

"Yeah, I have the chain. The clasp broke, but the rest of it is fine. The twins said Tommy was going to come to see you.

I can wait and give it to him, okay? One of your team should keep it for you."

"Yes. Tommy can fix it. That works." Mackey kept hold of his hand, refusing to let go.

He understood. He wasn't sure how he knew but it seemed like everything he needed to know, at least right now, was in Mackey's eyes. "Close your eyes and rest. I'm going to stay, Mackey. Okay? I'll stay at least until Tommy can get here, and then he will stay. You won't be alone."

"Okay. Yeah. If I'm asleep when Doc comes back, you'll tell him I need to go home?"

"I'll tell him you said so. Sure, Mackey." Not that it would do the cowboy one damn bit of good. He squeezed Mackey's fingers. "It's all good, man. Go to sleep."

"All good." Mackey sighed softly, and it didn't take long for the ring to fall from Mackey's free hand.

Sid scooped it up from the sheets and put it back in his pocket with the chain. As Mackey's hand went slack in his, it was his turn not to want to let go. He let himself puzzle over the feeling, telling himself it was just sympathy. It wasn't anything weird, it shouldn't make him uncomfortable.

But he dropped Mackey's hand like a hot potato when Doc came through the curtain again, covering by running his fingers over the bed railing. *Shit.*

"Oh good. He needed to rest. He's going up for a CAT scan in a bit to check for a brain bleed."

"I don't know, Doc. He was groggy, but I don't think it was his head. He told a pretty coherent story about his granddad." Sid grinned at Doc. "Oh, he did ask me to tell you that he needs to go home."

"Of course he did. He'll be at the event tomorrow, if he's not tied down here, mark my words."

"Tied down? That'll be enough? I was thinking horse tranquilizer."

"Oh, you're quick on your feet. That's an excellent suggestion. Needs must when the devil drives, huh?"

Sid nodded. "Are you really going to clear him to work? You could just... not."

"If they let him go back to the hotel, he'll be at work. He showed up to an event three days after he was released from his last broken neck. Mackey's whole life is protecting the guys -- his team and the cowboys. There's nothing else -- no family, nothing."

Sid frowned and watched Mackey sleeping, letting everything Doc had just said sink in--really sink in--and put more pieces of Mackey's puzzle together in his head. He didn't need to ask why anymore, at least not for Mackey.

"I promised him I would stay. At least until Tommy can get here. I'll give Tommy the ring to hold for him." He didn't know how to tell Doc he got it; he hoped maybe that would be enough.

"That would be a blessing. I'm going to harangue ER docs."

He waited for Doc to leave and then took Mackey's hand again, tucking it between both of his.

12

Mackey missed the second night of the event, but by Sunday morning he was up and moving, one set of uniforms sent to the laundry, his second-best pair on his increasingly old body.

Tommy was there to fetch him with a breakfast burrito and a cherry limeade in hand, and he was practicing his stare on the nurses. "I got to go, honey. Get me them papers. Event starts at two. My boys warm up at noon."

"Just be patient, Mister Keyes. I have to wait for--"

Tommy stepped in front of her and leaned against the foot of his bed. "We understand, luv, of course we do, but-- oh. Would you look at that? The blue in that scarf truly brings out the color of your eyes."

And there was his ringer, ramping up the accent and turning on the Aussie charm. The nurse blinked at him, surprised.

"I--thank you."

"You're welcome. Listen, can I ask you a big favor? Mackey here is the best in the business. He's the anchor of our team, and we need him. I need him, you understand?"

"Oh. Well I--"

Tommy slipped an arm around her shoulders and walked her through the curtains. He was back in two minutes, grinning smugly. "Give her a few."

"You are good at that, son."

"I know, Mother. You got it, you got to flaunt it." Tommy flashed him a grin. "How's the head?"

"'Bout as good as them ribs." But they had a job to do, and goddamn it, they were fixin' to do it.

"Oi. They're not going anywhere. The boys and Fabiano did a good job of reminding me how old I am last night though." Tommy shook his head and leaned against the bed. "Those kids got between me and everything."

"Good. I'm sorry I couldn't be there. Doc had my ass strapped to the bed and a tube in my dick 'til six this morning." Fucker.

"All good. Doc knows what's best, and I prefer you alive, Mother. You work better that way." Tommy's crooked grin was less sarcastic this time. "I hate this arena."

"No shit on that. You think if we go on strike they'll listen?" He managed not to completely crack up, mainly because it would kill his head.

"You know it, mate. They'll listen to the sound of the door hitting us in the ass." Tommy chuckled gently, one hand on his side.

"Yeah. They give no shits about anything but lining their pockets, up at the top." Him and the others, they were replaceable, at least to the suits. The cowboys, though, they knew.

"You have the crowd though, Mother. They like you. That matters to the high-rollers. Anyways we don't need all of that. We just do our jobs and mind our own, am I right?"

"That's that, and you are. Where the fuck is that nurse? I

want to work this final and go home. I start driving at five tonight, I can be home at noon tomorrow, give or take." They were on the break after this event, and he was desperate for it. He needed to sit and sleep solid for a week, maybe ten days.

"You might want to think about that drive, Mother. Alone, with your head? Think hard." Tommy chuckled again. "If you're able."

The nurse came back in right then and smiled sweetly at Tommy. He'd have sworn he was the patient, but she seemed to look right past him. "Mister Keyes's paperwork is all set. He just needs to sign, and you can take him home."

Tommy took the clipboard and put it in his lap. "Sign, mate. The pretty lady's got you out."

"Thank you, ma'am." He signed without looking. He had instructions and meds and all sorts of warnings. Whatever. He didn't have time to stress it. "Grab the burrito, Tommy. I'll eat it after. The drink's enough for now."

"I have a wheelchair coming; it'll just be a minute," the nurse said.

"Oh. Thank you, but you're walking, right, Mother? Press and all..."

"I don't think that's allowed..."

"Let's go, Tommy. You have a nice day, ma'am." Allowed? Fuck that. What were they fixin' to do?

"Follow me. I'll get you to my truck. I parked close." The little hitch in Tommy's walk disappeared as they headed out through the waiting room.

He kept his head down and walked, following Tommy's back like there was a leash attached. Just walk. He wasn't talking to anyone. At all.

Tommy had him covered, telling the cameras they'd be at the venue tonight and that was where they'd talk. Tommy unlocked the truck and got in, and as soon as he had his door shut, they were gone. "Not bad, Mother. You didn't even grunt at them." Tommy glanced over. "What's it gonna take tonight? I'll make sure the boys know."

"I'm going to have to try not to hit my head. I'll tell them I can't do the TV spot. I'll scare the kids." He was going to pray for an easy afternoon, because Lord knew he needed it.

"We could pull Fabi back in and tell them the arena is dangerous, and we need the extra man. Buck would back us up I bet." Tommy shrugged. "Then you could hang back a little."

"Bring Fabi in. We'll keep him close if we need him." That way the twins would be supported, no matter what.

"Got it. I'll have him run warm-up so we can be old and creaky for a bit. I'm not going to run for sure. We're ready for this break, hey?"

"Fuck yes. I've never been so tired, I don't think." In fact, he'd never felt so fucking old, and he'd been way more broke dick.

Tommy pulled into the parking lot at the hotel. "Quick change, and then we're off for the arena. Don't forget to check out."

They climbed out of the truck, each of them groaning as they shut the doors. "You got your room key?"

"I--It's in my gear. You have that?" Dammit. Dammit.

"Roigh. Yeah, I do. Hang on." Tommy unlocked the truck again and pulled out his bag, wincing a little at the reach. "Forgot."

"Careful, asshole." He would have grinned, but it hurt to do it, so he didn't bother. "Tell me the story about when we retire and live in splendid wealth again."

His gear seemed to levitate, Jack grabbing his shit. "Men

like us bleed out on the dirt or explode on the ranch, and we know it."

Tommy snorted. "Oi. Except if we have a fancy house and are sitting on retirement dough. Right, Mother?"

"Yep." He'd hit oil on the old family home in Abilene, and now his happy ass had a huge old house and a chunk of land in the Rockies. Somewhere he could see wild mustangs, elk, even a bear once.

Tommy peered around him at Jack. "You ready for break, mate? You have plans?"

"I do. Got a date with a beer and my binoculars. Not sure where yet, we'll see where the highway takes me later. Remind me where do we meet up next?"

"Us? Fort Worth for the big stock show. We got a show in South Dakota that Jaime's riding." Jack didn't drive his horses that far. Hell, the son of a bitch was on a borrowed mount for this event, because Dub was working a local event in El Paso.

"Save me from them northerners." Jack chuckled and held the lobby door for them. "You headed to your place, Mackey?"

"Yeah, I'm driving up as soon as the event's over."

"He thinks he is. That's a long drive for a guy with a head… thing." Tommy pointed to his own head and nodded meaningfully at Jack.

"Stop it. I done worse." At least he thought he had. "I need to go home. Bad."

"You want me to follow you up, Mother?" Tommy was probably headed to the beach, like always. West, not north, so his place was way out of Tommy's way.

"No, son. I got this. I'll stop if I need to. You go rest and recreate. I'm going to sleep a lot." He was going to watch elk and try to remember being twenty.

Jack shrugged. "I'd come up, but I've got to go check on my horses. You just take the drive easy, Mack."

They got on the elevator and the doors closed. "How many guys will be hanging at your place this time, Mother, do you even know?"

"None, that I know of. I didn't invite no one, but you know how that is." Guys showed -- they were lonely, bored, broke, hurting, heartsore -- and they came to heal.

"My money's on Parker."

"Not a chance." Tommy laughed. "Mackey would eat him alive."

Jack followed them off the elevator. They waved Tommy off, and Jack carried his bag for him all the way to his room. "I just checked out. You need a hand? How about I hang out and wait for you?"

"Yeah. Yeah, if you don't mind." He was fixin' to start puking, and he didn't want Tommy seeing.

Jack followed him in. "Tommy's right, you know. Driving alone is a bad idea. I'm not going to tell you what to do, but I'd look for a driving buddy."

"Maybe. Maybe so." He nodded, and shit, wasn't that a mistake? He made it to the bathroom before losing it, but it was a close thing. Fuck a doodle goddamn doo.

He heard the TV turn on. "I'm eating your pork rinds!" Jack was made of fucking stone; nothing got to him, and it was good to know someone was there.

Crawling to the shower made him incredibly grateful he always asked for a handicapped accessible room. Sometimes his legs didn't want to work, and sometimes his head didn't.

13

"Can I take your headset, boss?"

Sid blinked. "Oh. Yeah." He pulled it off and handed it to Gus. "Nice work tonight."

He hoped.

Sid had worked the last half hour of the show distracted. He got the job done; he didn't drop any cues or fuck anything up, but his mind hadn't been totally in the game, either. Like when he used to commute to work on the subway every morning, and he'd space the trip thinking about work or a date or just letting his mind wander while people watching, and suddenly the doors would open at his stop, and he'd hop up and hurry off the train wondering how the hell he'd gotten there so fast.

Jesus he was so ready for this break.

"Thanks." Gus hung out in the doorway. "You okay? You headed out tonight?"

"No. I've got my room for tonight. I'll head out tomorrow."

"Okay. Well, have a good break, man. I'll see you in... what? New York? Connecticut?"

"That's the rumor."

Gus gave him a fist bump and left him alone in the booth.

He was tired, but Tommy and Mackey looked fried. It was hard to believe either of them had made it through the afternoon. Sid had been worried about Mackey the whole damn night, and he didn't even know why. How was Mackey even his business? The bull fighters had Buck and Cody... they weren't his worry.

Sid headed out, turning off the lights in the control room and walking through the half-dark arena. He was about to pull out his keys when he noticed the light on in the locker room. He was thinking he should turn it off, and then the sound of someone being violently ill was sudden and loud.

What the hell?

He lingered there a second, caught between none of his business, and maybe he should see if he could help. The cowboys called him a "suit" most of the time and really didn't want anything to do with him, but he'd promised himself, after Mackey nearly passed out looking for that ring, that he wasn't going to walk away anymore. He took a step toward the doorway, squinting in the bright light and then decided fuck it, if whoever was in there didn't need his help, they could kick him out, but he was going to be the good guy and at least check on them.

If he had a dollar for every time he'd said "fuck it", he'd be a rich man instead of just a stupid one.

This time it turned out he wasn't so stupid after all. He found Mackey on the floor, naked as a jaybird and pale as a sheet, puking his lungs out.

"Jesus. Mackey?" He moved around behind the bull fighter to stay out of the puke and put a hand on Mackey's back. Mackey's skin was clammy and felt cool even though

Mackey looked like he was burning up. Sid looked around for something to cover him up.

"Headache. Sorry." Mackey tried to sit up, swaying dangerously as he did.

"Headache?" He snagged a folded towel from one of the benches, then pulled out his phone. "I'm calling Doc."

"No. No. No, now. I'm fine. I'll just--" Mackey blinked at him. "Just a headache. You let me get this cleaned up, and I'll sleep it off in the truck."

His thumb hovered over Doc's number. "It's not just a headache. Look at you. Has this been going on all night? I need to get you looked at."

"I cain't. I cain't let no one know. I'm okay. I got this..." Mackey tried to stand, fumbling to his knees.

"Whoa." Sid reached out and caught Mackey by the arm, steadying him. "Just... uh. Maybe the bench? Let me help." He shoved his phone back in his pocket and offered his other arm. "Easy okay? Careful."

"Thank you." Mackey was sheened with sweat, breathing hard, head down. "Fuckin' embarrassing."

"Fucking scary is more like it." He got it now. This time it was bad enough that Mackey was worried he'd lose his job over it. Why else hide it from Doc? "What the hell am I looking at here?" Sid did his best to cover the man in the towel again. Even pale and sick as a dog Mackey was built like a fucking Adonis.

"Just a sick headache. No big."

No big? Naked and puking on the floor was no big?

"I know better. You know I know better, right? I'm not an idiot." He sighed. There was more conversation to be had, but he couldn't just stand here anymore, and it fucking reeked in the locker room. "Can you shower? I'll find a... like a mop or something."

"Yeah. Yeah, I'm sorry. I'll get it. I was tryin'."

"I know. It's cool, I've got it." He looked Mackey over again. "Do you...would you like a hand getting to the showers?"

"You mind? Falling got me down there."

"Of course." Sid didn't let himself think too hard about it, just reached for Mackey, pulled him to his feet and got a supportive arm around behind the very naked man's back. "Lean on me."

"God, you're a good man. I appreciate it."

"You're welcome." Anyone would help Mackey, wouldn't they? He'd seen it happen with that ring. Still, he didn't breathe much as he got Mackey into the shower; the man smelled a little like death. "Be honest, do you need me to stand here and make sure you don't fall? If not I'll go clean up."

"No. No, I got this. I'll be right out to clean up. You've been sweet as all get out."

Okay. Good. Sid gave Mackey a hard look. "Be careful. Okay? Call out if you need help."

"Yessir. I got this. Thank you ever so." The curtain closed, and the water started.

Sid stared at the closed shower curtain. It was hard to believe that the man in the shower was the same one whose eyes had shot hot daggers at him not so long ago. He turned and went on the hunt for a mop wondering how often Mackey got the headaches and for how long. Was this just from the current injury? And did no one else know? He was all alone; surely if someone understood it was this bad they wouldn't have left Mackey on his own.

Legally speaking, he didn't know either. He would be obligated to call Doc if he knew Mackey was that ill, and he had no intention of getting Mackey fired.

He found a mop and custodial pail pretty easily and was almost done cleaning up when he heard the water shut off.

Mackey came out in jeans and a t-shirt, the clothes skimming him and just hinting at that ripped belly. "Hey. Sorry about that. You didn't need to see that."

Damn. How was it that some men were hot naked but somehow even hotter wearing just the right T-shirt? "No. I didn't. But you needed some help so I'm glad I did."

"I did. I'm embarrassed as hell, but you're right." Mackey sighed softly and pulled on his coat. "You headed out tonight?"

"No. No, I have a room. One more night for me. I was going to leave from the arena, but I--can't."

"I hear that. I'm not sure I'll be going as far as I wanted, you know?"

"Yeah, for sure. I was going to call an Uber, but maybe I could grab a ride? I just need to put this thing back where I got it." *Ask him what's up with the headaches. Just ask.* He stuffed the mop into the bucket and started to roll it toward the door.

"I don't guess you'd be interested in driving?"

"Well, I'm interested in getting to the hotel in one piece so, yeah. I'll drive." Sid had questions. The car was a good place to ask, right? Back when they got along, Dad would take him for a drive when they needed a talk. Now, Sid called every Sunday instead. Dad would pretend not to want to talk to him and then talk anyway. Bullshit mostly, about the neighbors, or politics, or sports, or his bad foot... anything to keep Sid on the phone for a bit.

Sid stashed the bucket where he'd found it and pointed to a wide doorway, fluorescent lighting pouring into the darker hall. "You might want to tuck that hat down; it's bright in the exit corridor."

"Thanks." Mackey hid in his hat brim, head down.

"Mhm." The last thing he wanted was more sick cowboy.

He led Mackey down the long hallway and out the exit doors that led to the parking lot. The few vehicles that were left were covered in a very light dusting of snow, reminding him this was a holiday break they were on. He tugged his coat collar up higher. "Hey, snow in Vegas! How often does that happen?" Almost never, he'd bet. Sid took it as a sign that he was doing the right thing. They got to the truck, and he stuck his hand out. "You want to give me your keys?"

"Yeah." Mackey handed them over, then put his gear in the bed. "I owe you. Big."

Sid shook his head. "No. No you don't. I'm glad I could help." They climbed into the truck, and he futzed with the seat so his knees weren't wedged under the steering wheel. "I'm curious what's up though. If anybody asks me, I don't know anything...but I'd like to know what I don't know. Is this new or...?"

"I got a broken neck a while back, and headaches came with it, never went away. But this damn thing--" He motioned to his chin. "Fuck. It's harsh."

He was never going to get used to that, was he? How casually these men talked about broken necks, head injuries, busted pelvises. How this horrifying set of stitches was just another day at the office.

"Are they always this bad?" He knew the way to the hotel by now, and just got going. It was a comfy truck. Definitely lived-in, but he liked the way it drove.

The radio was tuned to the country Sirius channels, there was a place on the dash for a cellphone, and in the gun rack, there was a fishing pole.

"No. Not always. It's just a headache. Nobody ever died from one, right?"

He glanced over at Mackey. "You're joking right? That isn't just a headache. I guess you haven't told anyone they get this bad? I'm surprised you were alone." Alone was bad enough; working was worse. A bull could easily have gotten the better of Mackey with a headache like that. Shit, with both Mackey and Tommy hurt, someone could have died.

"It ain't no big deal. I just fell, you know? Hit my head." Mackey's head was down, and he could read shame and worry.

All right. It was time to back off. This was bigger than some broken bones...closer to home. Mackey obviously knew damn well what he was doing and had made his choices, so until Sid had a good reason to needle the man about it, he decided to leave it alone. Mackey was doing his best not to look as sick as he must feel, and Sid figured he'd just keep the guy entertained until they got to the hotel. "Do you feel any better? Do you have something you can take for this? Maybe something to help you get some rest?"

"I got shit from the ER. I am going to get some Sprite and some soup, and... well, I'm getting on the road in a bit."

"On the road? Like this?"

"I want to go home. Bad. It's only sixteen-seventeen hours from here."

"Oh." Sid didn't know what to say to that. He didn't think Mackey would make it an hour on the road, but then he hadn't thought Mackey would stay on the dirt all afternoon either, and he'd been wrong about that, hadn't he?

Doc said Mackey's life was protecting the guys. *There's nothing else,* the man had said. What Doc hadn't mention was what Sid was thinking right now, but Sid had seen it— the look in Mackey's eyes when Tuff Nut came for him... it seemed like Mackey was more than willing to die on the dirt.

Yeah. He didn't trust himself to say anything, so he just drove. Mackey must've felt the tension and changed the subject.

"You heading home for the break?"

He shook his head. "I'd planned to go home, visit my dad but... that didn't work out." Dad had cancelled last minute, saying it wasn't a good time. That probably meant his big brother Lance was going to be there with his family. Plan B was to stay with friends in New York, but that hadn't panned out either. So at this point, he was going to rent a car tomorrow and pick a place that was a seven or eight hour drive away and go there. Santa Fe maybe. Route 66.

"No? I'm sorry. Tommy offered to help me get home, but-" Mackey started to shrug, then swallowed a soft groan. "He was heading to the beach for the holidays. He's never gotten used to Christmas in the snow."

Sid glanced at Mackey. Was Mackey admitting he couldn't make it home on his own? Was he asking for help driving? Would it be weird if Sid offered?

For the second time tonight Sid decided fuck it and offered. "I'd totally drive you."

Mackey glanced at him. "I got me a big ole house in the mountains. You'd be able to rest there. It'll be a winter wonderland."

"I've heard about it; everybody says it's gorgeous up there. I'm in. I've got a room until tomorrow. We can get some sleep, have breakfast, and then get on the road." Of course he said that, and now he couldn't remember if the little loveseat thing in his room folded out. He only had a king bed.

As he pulled into the parking lot, he promised himself he wasn't going to make things awkward. It was just a bed. Just sleep.

"I can see if they got another room, if me crashing in yours cramps your style."

"Pfft." He laughed as he parked the truck. "I have no style." Of course, Mackey could afford one and, if they had one, why would Mackey want to share? "I mean, I don't care one way or the other. You want to see if they have a room?"

"I'll ask at the front desk."

Sid couldn't help but hope they were full up. Mackey didn't need to be alone after a fall, a night in the hospital, and not being able to get up off the floor.

He'd worry all night.

He couldn't have that. Right?

Sid grabbed Mackey's bag for him from the back of the truck. The lobby was busy as hell when they went in, loud with conversation. "Wow."

"Jesus. Look at all of them." Mackey kept his head down, wincing from the noise.

They got in the line at reception but there were six or eight people in front of them. "Are you okay to wait in this line?"

"I--"

No. No, this was not okay with him. This was dangerous, unhealthy, and flat out wrong. He hooked a hand around Mackey's hips and started moving toward the elevators. "Come on. We can share, or we can call down from my room."

"Yeah. Yeah, I'm a little...Yeah, thank you. You're good people." That Mackey followed proved that the man was dragged through the dirt.

He literally propped Mackey up against the wall in the elevator. "Are your meds in your bag?"

"Yeah. Was going to save them for after my drive."

"You should take them. You can crash all night, sleep in

the truck tomorrow. Whatever you need." If he was doing this, he was doing it right. He'd try to help Mackey heal up before this whole insanity started again.

"Yeah. I might have to. I'll buy your supper, get me some Sprite and a bowl of chicken soup to take the pills with."

"You got it." He let Mackey into his room, which he remembered too late was a total mess. He started picking up clothing and kicking shoes back into the closet. "Sorry. I'm a slob. Just... sorry. They made the bed, so go ahead and relax."

"No worries. Sometimes I room with the twins, remember?" There was a hint of twinkle in Mackey's eyes.

"God, I can't even imagine." Sid laughed and sat Mackey's bag down on the little loveseat at one end of the room. "I have some uh... I think..." Sid opened the little fridge and pulled out a Gatorade. "Yep. They stock these in my room everywhere I go. They must be a sponsor or something." He handed it to Mackey and grinned. "It's... blue flavor."

"Ah, yes. The refreshing blue. Purple is nowhere near as nice."

"It's better than the green. The green tastes... exactly how it looks. Like pee." Sid hung their coats up, then kicked off his boots and dug a pair of sweats out of the pile of clothing he'd just scooped up off the floor. "I'm starving. Let me find the room service menu; it's too much of a zoo in that lobby to brave it again."

"Yessir. Thank you for letting me come sit. Hell, thank you for...well, my ring, the ride, everything. Tommy told me how good you were to me."

"I was happy to help, especially after you told me all about why the ring is so important to you. Honestly, people came out of the woodwork to help find it; it was just luck that it ended up in my hand."

"Still, it means the world." Mackey tried to smile, but Sid could see how it hurt.

"You're welcome." Sid gave him a nod and dug up the room service book. "Soup, you said?" He sat on the end of the bed, careful not to jostle it too much. "Chicken, right?"

"Yessir. Chicken soup and Sprite, please." Mackey glanced at him. "You mind terrible much if I take my boots off?"

"I don't know too many people who sleep with them on." Sid chuckled, nose in the menu. "Mine are long gone. Please. Get comfy."

"Thanks." Mackey slipped the boots off and settled, face relaxing as he leaned back.

Beat to hell, sick as a dog, stitches in his chin, and circles under his eyes...and somehow Mackey was still...

Sid blinked and stared back at his menu. He was a little infatuated, dammit. And he shouldn't be. There wasn't a worse idea in the history of the planet. Even if they didn't work together, that cowboy wanted nothing to do with a "suit".

He sighed and picked up the phone, looking anywhere but at the bull fighter stretched out on his bed. He sat on hold for a bit but eventually got through, ordered Mackey's soda and soup and he went for a burger and a beer.

"Oh, do they have ice cream, honey?"

"Oh wait! Sorry... have you got ice cream?" He looked at Mackey. "What kind?"

"Chocolate? Vanilla if that's what they have."

Sid asked for chocolate for Mackey, and strawberry for himself and hung up. "Good call on the ice cream, and I don't even have a good excuse like you do. You want to watch a movie?"

"Sure, honey. Just nothing scary, please. Pain pills give me nightmares sometimes."

"Gotcha." He dug around for the remote but didn't find it. "So... what's your favorite thing about your house?"

"Would you believe that I'm not sure? I haven't even been in all the rooms yet." Mackey chuckled softly. "I love the view from the balcony in my bedroom. There's a loft in the front room too, that looks out into the mountains, the pond."

Whoa. "You haven't been--what? Are you serious? How long have you had the place again?"

"I bought it in July. So, almost five months? But I've only been back a half dozen times, maybe ten? It was a wreck -- still is. So I go back, clean, go back, clean. It's a great place. Great bones. But I have a lot of work to make it a...sanctuary."

"I've never thought about buying a place. I just... rent. I've never figured out where I should land for good, because I move around so much for work. Even before this job. My place in New York is nice, but it's never going to be a sanctuary." Not even close. He loved the city; there was always something going on somewhere no matter the hours he was working, but he hoped he wouldn't be there forever. He'd find a home someplace. Eventually.

"This is my first purchase. I inherited the family land, so this is going to be the first time I get to make something my own."

"That's good, right? Making it your own? Seems like something to look forward to."

"Very much. It's...God, it's this massive place. I can't tell you. There's wood everywhere, but the rooms need to be redone. I've done the kitchen, the outside kitchen, and the guest room all the way. That's it." Mackey was rambling a little, and it was adorable.

"Sounds like you could use a hand. Maybe you should ask all those freeloaders that drop by when you're not home." Sid snorted. Just what Mackey needed, a bunch of random cowboys working unsupervised. The remote was sticking out from under the foot of the bed. "Ah! Found it."

Mackey applauded for him. "They're just kids, you know? Boys. They need a safe place where they can come and not be at their folks'."

Sid nodded, looking at the remote and flipping it over in his fingers. "Yeah. I remember that." He rolled his eyes and turned the TV on. "Sort of."

"Yeah. I don't."

The bald words shocked the hell out of him.

Sid was about ask how and when Mackey had lost his parents when there was a knock at the door. "Dinner."

Just as well; that was a nosy question.

Still, he wanted to know how a man that seemed like the most paternal man on earth could say that. His best guess was that it wasn't true.

"You ready to eat?" Sid let room service in. They set down a big tray on the desk and left after he signed the ticket. "It's tempting to start with the ice cream, right?"

"Let's do. The rest can wait." Mackey shot him a wink.

"Right on." Sid found the chocolate and a spoon and handed it over, then grabbed his strawberry and flopped on the other side of the bed with it. "I have a microwave. We can zap anything that gets cold."

"Perfect." Mackey took a colorful handful of pills, then began to eat the ice cream in little princess bites, not opening his mouth.

"That's a lot of meds. You're going to sleep well. I think if I needed that much medication I'd still be in the hospital crying like a big baby." He flipped channels. "*Young Frankenstein*, have you seen it? I love this movie."

"Oh, hell yeah. Gene Wilder was a damn genius." Mackey ate another bite. "I hate hospitals. I just needed to get out. Walked out twelve hours after they replaced my femur."

Sid chuckled. "Yeah, but you might be insane. Jury is still out on that one."

"Might? Shit, 'm a bull fighter. We're batshit crazy."

That got a full out laugh. "Yeah. That's been my impression. But you gave me permission to eat ice cream first, so you're okay in my book."

"Life is short, honey. Dessert first."

True enough for a bull fighter he supposed, so he ate every bite of it and drank up what had melted in solidarity while they giggled through the movie.

Mackey leaned against him, getting heavier and heavier. Sid wanted Mackey to fall asleep, so he wasn't sure why he felt so awkward about it. It was kind of adorable. Mackey's giggles during the movie had been pure joy, and yeah, he loved the smell of a man fresh out of the shower. But so what?

He took Mackey's bowl and set it with his own on the nightstand. He should get up and deal with the food, right? He should grab a shower. He could just tuck Mackey in, no big deal.

"You smell good, honey." Mackey sighed softly, ninety nine percent asleep.

Oh, that--well, that was the drugs talking. This was his second encounter with the drugged-up bull fighter, and he knew this time what Mackey needed to hear. Still, his cheeks went hot, and he was glad Mackey was too sleepy to notice. "Thanks. You can fall asleep, Mackey. It's okay. I'm not going anywhere."

"Thank you." Mackey squeezed his fingers, then held on, just sinking into the pillows.

That'd be a cool trick if he could make it work, like, at a bar or something. Or when Mackey was in adrenaline mode.

He held Mackey's hand, keeping a firm grip. He was pretty stuck right where was for a while. He could be cool. Just hang out and watch some TV. It didn't matter that there was a hot cowboy in his bed, holding his hand.

One that thought he smelled good.

Just be chill.

He reached over and turned the light off, leaned back in the pillows and went back to watching Gene Wilder.

14

Mackey had never had a road trip that was more fun, and he'd been in a truck with Jack for years. He and Sid had Cokes and snacks, music, pillows...he was having a goddamn ball.

Weird. Wonderful though.

"I need some of those cheese crackers," Sid said. "Look at that big tree. It looks like a gnome with the snow all piled up like his beard."

"Gnomes ain't big, honey." He dug up the Cheez-Its and handed the box over.

"Shut up. You're supposed to be tough not smart." Sid grinned over at him. "Do they put crack in these cheese things?"

"Yep. But there ain't no calories on road trips. No worries." He cackled, digging up one of the Ding Dongs.

"Easy on the chewing; you're on pain meds remember. Oh, I love this song!" Sid turned the radio up and started singing and drumming on the steering wheel. Sid was pretty confident about his voice and had reason to be.

He sang along, nice and low, not interrupting Sid's song.

Lord have mercy, he thought maybe someone was about as ready to be on a good, long break as he was.

Sid turned the song down about halfway in, and his low voice was suddenly loud. "Ooh. You can sing." Sid stuck a hand in the box of Cheez-Its again.

"Yeah, not really, but I love the music. All sorts." He was having a goddamn ball, hurting as much as he was.

"Me too. I've got pretty broad taste. Except opera. I'm not so good with opera."

"Ah yes. The oodle-oodles. Not my thing, but to each his own." He didn't need them weird hats with horns, although...That would be damn funny for next Halloween. He'd get all of them some.

"Oodles? Ha. That's great. So, did you figure out where you want to stop for the night, or are we winging it?"

"You want to try Jackson Hole? It's fine there, and we could get something decent." He loved this – travelling with someone, taking it easy. "And right now it's lit up like magic for Christmas."

"Sounds great, I've never been. Mountains there, right? Should be snowier than where we were."

Sid's cell phone rang, and he took one hand off the wheel to grab it, but it had slid down the dashboard to Mackey's side. "It's by you. Does it say who's calling?"

Mackey reached for it and the screen lit up. "Says 'Brad Cambridge'." He didn't wrinkle his nose, but mainly only because it hurt to do it. Him and Brad had history -- like broke neck history, but that wasn't none of Sid's.

Sid sighed. "Put it on speaker, and don't say a word." Sid looked at him. "Please."

"You got it, honey." He answered and clamped his mouth shut.

"Hey, Brad. I'm driving. What's up?"

"Sid. Where are you headed?"

Sid glanced at Mackey and then back at the road.

"Jackson Hole. Why?"

"Yeah? Nice up there. What the hell happened at the arena? We didn't need a bunch of bullshit at the final round."

Mackey could see Sid's fingers grip the steering wheel. "We had a great show. Some cowboys earned some money. What are you after, Brad?"

"Well, Sid. I'd heard there was some drama with the bull fighters and Mack Keyes, and I'm just making the rounds trying to piece it together."

"Did you watch the replay? He got Jack's rope in the face Friday night – you were still there, right? Then he was back Sunday for the short go. That's about all I know."

"That's it? I was told you went to the hospital."

Sid rolled his eyes. "Oh that? He'd lost something in the dirt, and I brought it to him, that was it."

There was a long silence on the line and Sid looked at him and shrugged. Mackey grinned over, pantomimed crying. Brad was dying for him to fuck up and get himself fired. Wasn't going to happen. Not a chance.

"Is he losing control of the bull fighters?" Brad asked, and Mackey closed his eyes to keep the laughter in.

Control? Tommy? Shee-it. He had a chance with the twins, but it was a teeny shot. Like a thread. They worked together because they respected each other, and because they were the best. No question.

"Brad, I'm just a camera jockey. What the hell do I know about bull fighters? All I know is they're lunatics, and the wrecks make good TV. Did you ask Buck or Cody?"

"I did."

"Good. I gotta run, Brad. Driving is hairy in the

mountains, and a snowstorm just started. Have a good night." Sid nodded at him to hang up.

"Good night, Sid. Drive Sa--"

Sid laughed as Mackey cut Brad off. "Bye-bye."

"See you, asshole!" Mackey howled with laughter, even if it pulled shit that didn't need pulling.

"What a dick. He basically admitted he was calling around for gossip. What did he think I was going to say? I may know what I know, but I'm not giving him any details that Buck or Cody didn't give him. You know, he told me a while back at dinner that I could threaten you with your job. What's his deal?"

"I forced him to retire." Simple as that. He'd brought Brad's career to a halt, and Brad wanted the same.

Sid looked at him sharply and then back at the road. "Whoa."

Mackey knew that wasn't going to be the end of that, though. He waited for the questions.

"Wait. How? That's gotta be a story."

"Yeah. Brad had a bit of a trouble with the bottle, and he showed up to ride one day, fucked up. We didn't know on the dirt, of course, and he was a biggie-wow, so no one said boo. Not until he hit the dirt and was too drunk to get back up. We lost Clay Michaels that day, and I broke my neck." He'd damn near hit the ground with his Clay and not got back up, neither, but that wasn't the cowboy way. "I didn't sue the league, and neither did Clay's daddy, but Brad retired."

Sid squinted at him, but it took him a minute to say anything. "Retired. But he's now... on the board? And he's got it out for you." Sid nodded like it was all clear as day.

"All the original guys are on the board. That won't

change." And he could have it out all he wanted; Mackey didn't care. He was who he was, full stop.

"He hosts a dinner for the corporate side once a month. I went a while ago. I think I'm going to be busy for the next one. No wonder Cody got up and walked out. It's a wonder he goes at all."

"Cody's a tough bastard, but fair. We ain't friends, but I respect him, trust him with my boys." And God help the bastard tried to ride drunk with Cody. He'd tear it up.

"He's got your back. That much I can tell you for sure." Sid pointed. "This is the weirdest drive. We're in Utah, then Wyoming for like a second, then back in Utah, now back in Wyoming again..."

"Yeah. We're wandering. Tomorrow we'll head straight down, but today we'll see the things." He glanced over, grinned. "You having fun?"

"I am." Sid's smile seemed young, relaxed. "I love to drive for one thing, I love road trips, and I just really needed to get away from work for a bit." He shook his head.

"Yeah. Yeah, I hear you. It was time for a break. For a change of scenery." And a rest. He needed a rest.

"I can handle the work, and it's not like I'm burned out, it's kind of everything else. The learning curve has been steep, and I didn't think too hard about what living in hotels for months at a time would be like." Sid glanced over. "Did I tell you they offered me the job again, for next year?"

"You didn't, but it doesn't surprise me none." Sid knew how to work, no question. "Living in a hotel, though. That's a weird thing, yessir. I been doing it my whole adult life. Did you usually work in New York, then? Get to go home at night?"

"Yeah, I used to. I had a commute on the subway and everything. I was thinking about talent management actually; that's where my degree is. But I like the hands on better."

"I ain't never been on a subway. I think you do a damn good job, swear to God." They'd had words, but everyone did. They worked a tough goddamn job. Screaming was part of it.

Sid seemed a little surprised by that comment, but all he said was, "Thank you."

He nodded once and handed Sid a Ding Dong. They were pretty fresh.

"Seriously? More junk food?" Sid took it though. "How are you feeling? Like, no bullshit."

"Feel like I took a rope to the face and like I got twenty-eight stitches, a broke rib, and a bruise on my brain, but I ain't at work."

"Awesome." Sid shook his head in sympathy first, but then broke out in the giggles. "So, it's a good day."

"Fucking amazing," he agreed. "Top. Notch."

"I don't know how you're awake, with all those meds you're taking. You did sleep well last night though I guess."

"I did. Like the dead." He loved that, how Sid didn't know that you could hurt bad enough that no amount of pain pills could knock you out. It was dear.

"Is that our exit? Oh thank God." Sid pulled into the exit lane. "I mean, I like you and all, but I need out of this truck."

He'd gotten them a decent hotel room suite, something big enough to share but have space. And the lodge was nice without being uncomfortable.

Sid followed his directions, and before long the lodge came into view. It was something else -- a big old wooden rustic-looking place, with Christmas lights and sparkles, the chimneys all smoking away. The snow was falling, and it was a little like Santa's workshop. Sid's eyes went wide.

"Holy crap, Mackey. Look at this place! It's gorgeous. Not exactly a budget travel guy, huh?"

"They gave me a good rate. I'm here at least a couple times a year." He worked the Shiners rodeo for free, and he'd show up for a hoot when he was passing through.

"I feel spoiled. This beats the pants off the Best Western I was eyeballing in Santa Fe." Sid pulled up to the front entrance. They didn't have a lot of stuff, but his bag was heavy.

"If we're going to relax, we ought to relax. Do you have swim trunks? I might get in the water. I just can't get my stitches wet." He loved the pool here -- it was quiet, nice, indoors and heated.

"I do actually. I figured when I left New York that some of the hotels we've stayed in would have nice pools. I haven't actually found the time to swim, but I have trunks."

Sid climbed out of the truck and found his bag, hauling it out of the back. "Hang on. I'll grab yours too."

"I'll carry it, if you can lift it." The way his head throbbed when he lifted something heavy scared him.

Sid stared at him. "Really? Is it--"

"Mr. Keyes, we heard you were checking in." A valet rolled up with a luggage cart. "Welcome. Can I get your bags?"

"Hey there, Nicky. How's it going?" He was lucky; he had a knack for names.

"Good. Good, sir. I saw the wreck on the TV. You're okay?"

"Gonna have another scar, but it'll be sexy, right?"

"Ladies love scars. And you have another good story to go with it." Nicky took the bags and set them on the cart.

Mackey chuckled softly. He wasn't sure there were ladies

looking, but a few guys were about that still watched, so he'd take it.

"Mackey!" Gene, the hotel manager, came up and hugged him. "Jesus, what a wreck! I have your regular room. I'm so glad you stopped in. Headed home, are you?"

"I am. When are you coming to see me? Let me introduce you to my friend, Sid."

Gene stuck out his hand enthusiastically. "Welcome! Any friend of Mackey's..." Gene gave Sid a wink.

Sid's startled look was hilarious as he shook Gene's hand. "Thank you. This is a treat."

Gene put an arm around Mackey's shoulders and led him into the lobby. "What time for dinner? You want a special table?"

"Just nothing too hard to eat? I'm having a hell of a time opening wide."

Gene arched one eyebrow laughter written in every line of the man's face. "Pity."

"Now, Gene..." They both cracked up.

They stopped at the front desk, where a young woman behind the counter handed him two room cards with shaking hands. "Enjoy your stay, Mr. Keyes."

Nicky was already on the way to the elevator with their luggage, and Sid was handing off his truck keys to another young man in a valet uniform.

Mackey nodded to her, taking her hand and patting it, glancing at her name tag. "Nice to meet you, Miss Hannah. You're new here, hmm? You'll see me now and again. This is my favorite place to hang my hat when I'm not home."

She blushed a dark pink and smiled at him. "Thank you, sir. It's a special place. Very good to meet you too."

Gene tapped his shoulder as he turned away. "That's my

granddaughter," he whispered. "She doesn't like me to say so around guests though."

"Oh, Gene...She's as pretty as the day is long. Good on her, joining the family business." He shook his head. "I can't believe you've got one old enough to come work. You joining us for supper?"

"I can't believe it either. And if your *friend* doesn't mind, I'd be happy to."

"Sid, you mind company for supper? Gene's a decent sort, for someone not from Texas."

Gene laughed gently.

"Not at all, sounds great. I just need a shower first so I don't smell like a bull fighter." Sid winked at him, grinning.

"Why don't we meet down here around eight? You can get a shower and a nap."

"That would be a kindness, yes. Thank you." He could stretch out a little bit, breathe.

Sid nodded. "Thank you so much."

Gene gave them a wave and left them at the elevators.

It wasn't two seconds before Sid glanced at him. "Regular room, huh?"

He shrugged one shoulder, going for casual. "I been here a couple times."

"How about Jackson Hole,' he says. We could get something 'decent,' he says..." Sid laughed.

"Hey, this is decent, right? Nice suite. Good firm beds. Great bathroom..." He managed a wink. It was good to be him.

Sid snorted a laugh. "Oh, I'm all about a decent bathroom." They stepped off the elevator where Nicky waited for them by the door to be let in. Sid was looking around like he was in a museum or a palace. "Whoa. This is amazing."

"I do love it here." He gave Nicky a generous tip and a smile. "It's a good place, good people."

"Thank you, Mister Keyes." Nicky smiled back and left with the empty cart.

"Okay. This is nuts. Look at this room!" Sid went straight for the fireplace and turned on the gas, grinning like a kid with a new toy as it lit up. "There's a whole little holiday diorama. This is adorable."

He chuckled and landed on the leather sofa, letting it hold him in all the right places. "It's good to have a name."

"It's good to have a friend that has a name." Sid waggled his eyebrows and headed for the fridge. "There's beer! Ooh. But I need a nap. So later. But… there's beer."

"Tell me it's Shiner."

"It's Shiner. It's three kinds of Shiner. You know I'd never had Shiner until I took this job?" Sid closed the fridge and sank into the couch next to him, eyes on the fire. "Oh, hello couch."

"Right? It's like the best couch ever, barring mine." His had magic fingers and two reclining ends.

"I'll be sure and give you a review of yours too." Sid sighed, settling deeper into the couch. "I should shower." Sid didn't look like he was going anywhere.

"We got three hours." He was staying right here.

Sid's eyes closed. "Mhm…good. 'M nap."

He nodded. That worked for him. Nap. Snow out there being all pretty. Quiet. Goodness.

Hell yeah.

15

Most hotel pools had a rule about drinks and bottles on the deck, but it was late, and there wouldn't be kids around. In fact, Sid figured there probably wouldn't be anyone around at this hour. He set the two Shiners he'd opened in their room down near the steps to the shallow end and dropped his towel over a chair.

"Are you a wade in slowly guy or a dive into the deep end guy?" Personally, he was a cannonball guy, but that seemed... inappropriate here. The hotel was so stately and grown up, and obviously Mackey had a reputation with the management that Sid probably shouldn't mess with.

"Usually, I dive in, but with the stitches, I'm wading. Do what you will, honey. I judge not." Mackey wore bright blue shorts, the man's belly a washboard under dozens of scars.

Not that he'd noticed. He wasn't watching Mackey's ass as the bullfighter headed for the steps either. Nope. Just another cowboy, nothing to see here.

Gene had bought the drinks at dinner. He might have been a little buzzed.

"If you say so." Sid grinned and took off for the pool at a

run. He launched himself off the edge and landed with a splash, sinking a good way before uncurling and swimming back up to the surface. "Woo!" He laughed and shook the water from his hair. It had been a long, long time since he'd done that, and it felt great. "The water is fantastic."

"Nice and warm, huh?" Mackey floated at the edge of the pool, legs moving lazily.

"Yeah but not that gross warm, just the right warm." That made no sense. He knew what he meant, but no one else would. "You saw your beer there, right?"

"I did. You rock, thank you." Mackey moved away from the wall, drank deep, then settled again. "So, you like to swim."

He swam over and grabbed his beer. "I do. A lot. And I don't get to do it much, so this is a treat." It was a bummer about the stitches. He should probably have less fun since Mackey couldn't, right? He was being rude.

"Rock on. This is the best pool. Have at, honey. I'm going to float like a big, lazy log."

Sid watched Mackey stretch out so the water lifted him up. Aside from when the bullfighter was sound asleep on painkillers, this was the most relaxed he'd seen Mackey. The jaw thing wasn't so pretty right now, but the rest of the man was worth a second look. He took a big swig of his beer and set it down. "Just going to swim a little."

Sid glanced down the length of the pool, then took off at a slow crawl.

Every so often he looked over and, every time, Mackey's eyes were on him, the blue like a laser. He didn't think he'd ever had anyone watch him swim--or do anything really--that intensely. It was hard not to stare back.

It was hard not to wonder why the man was gazing.

It was even harder not to like it.

When Sid finally felt like he'd worked out the kinks from sitting in the truck and watching for patches of ice all day, he swam back over to his beer... and to Mackey. He was a little out of breath, but he felt good. "Having a good float?"

"I am. Enjoying the hell out of it, in fact."

Sid sipped his beer and watched the cowboy. The more time he spent with the guy the more he realized there wasn't anything he didn't like. He was getting a vibe; he wasn't oblivious, but he just couldn't figure out what Mackey was after.

They should be oil and water, so he wasn't sure what he was after either. Mackey's crowd wanted nothing to do with him, and he... didn't really have a crowd yet.

"Been a good day."

"It has been. You and Danny, you're really not a thing?" Okay, that came out of nowhere.

"Uh...no. We're definitely not. Never considered being a thing." He grinned at Mackey from behind his beer. "Never touched his thing."

"Good to know. I haven't touched his thing either. He's a sweet boy, but not my type."

"He's adorable but, like I told you before, I need a little more. He's been a good friend though." He put his beer down, thoughtfully. "Your type isn't Jack?"

"Jack's my friend, honey. A real good friend, sure."

There was nothing about the way Danny talked about Jack and Mackey that made him think they were together. He couldn't imagine... well, Jack seemed like a player. Mackey didn't.

"Why are we having this conversation?" In a noisy bar on a Saturday night that would have been a flirty question. Half-naked in a swimming pool with a hot cowboy it was a little more... calculated. "Are you looking for another good friend?"

"No. But I wanted to know if it was okay to watch. If you were taken, that would be nasty."

Ah. He laughed softly, embarrassed. He overshot that one, huh? Stuck his foot right in it. Go him. "I usually go with the *what they don't know doesn't hurt* theory." He tipped his beer up, finishing it.

"Yeah, but I'm old, I guess. I don't hunt 'em, they ain't mine to catch."

"Gentlemanly. I like it." He hauled himself up on the edge of the pool and sat, feet dangling in the water.

"Just how I was made." Mackey stayed in, up to his neck in the water.

"It's a shame you can't get that pretty face wet, I'm at the perfect angle here for a splash." He faked it, paddling his toes in the water.

"Shit, no one's thought I was pretty since I was sixteen and hoping to be a rock and roll star." Mackey snorted, hand snapping out snake-quick to snag his toe and tug.

He tugged back, but Mackey didn't let go. "No one's told you about your eyes?"

"What's wrong with my eyes?" Mackey went cross-eyed, making him chuckle. "Besides one being black, of course."

"It's not the black; it's the *blue*. Your eyes are beautiful, the way they shine. Like they have their own light. They're pretty." He shrugged. "You can go ahead and poke fun at that too, but it's true."

Mackey pinked and gave him a quirky little grin. "Thanks, honey. Seriously." He'd never heard that husky, pleased tone.

"You're welcome." He smiled back but the expression on

Mackey's face made him tingle, and his own cheeks warmed. He swallowed and looked down at his fingers.

Say something. Don't make it weird, say something.

"So what's the plan for tomorrow?"

"We'll head to the house. I'll order a bill of groceries to pick up on the way."

"Sounds good." He glanced back up at Mackie. "Make sure you get more Cheez-Its. I'm addicted now."

"You know it. I'm going to know you're a great road trip partner now too. I keep my people close." There was something special in the way Mackey said 'my people'.

"It was a fun drive. Long as hell, but fun. You know I like you when I'm willing to sing with you in the car." He winked, trying to keep a straight face and probably failing. "Not everybody gets a treat like that."

"I liked it. A lot." Mackey turned to get his beer, facing him this time. "There anything you want to do here tomorrow?"

Close-up all he could see now were those eyes. Clear and blue. "I don't know. What do people do up here besides look at the view? Which is amazing, by the way. Wow."

"There's skiing, snowboarding, snowmobiling -- all that stuff. In the summer there's rodeoin'." Mackey's hand was around his ankle, the calluses heavy and rough.

"No offense intended, but I'm a hard no on more rodeo for at least six weeks." He laughed. "I say we sleep in, have brunch with the view and then get moving. The drive has to be just as pretty, right?" Feeling bold, he stroked the back of Mackey's hand with his other foot. He didn't know what he was doing; he'd been fine until Mackey touched him. The firm grip the bullfighter had on his ankle confused him, made his heart beat heavily in his chest.

"It is. We can either go through Utah along the western

slope or over and down west of Denver. Either way, we'll be in God's country. It's a gorgeous drive, assuming you're not tired of driving in the snow." Mackey's thumb began to rub slow, easy circles.

"I love the snow, and they know how to handle it out here. I'm easy." He shifted his gaze to Mackey's fingers and then back again, offering Mackey a smile. "Most of the time."

"I'm not being skeezy, honey. I swear to God. You know that, right?"

"Mackey." Sid touched Mackey's shoulder. "I know." God, that was pure strength, a body made for taking damage and moving. Sid let his fingers explore the ridges of muscle there. "You're a good man. Anyone who knows you can see that."

Don't mix business with pleasure. Don't shit where you eat. Don't shoot holes in your own boat.

Jesus, Sidney. How about don't overthink this like you do everything else? The man has a hold of your ankle, not your dick.

Although he could imagine that, couldn't he? Those heavy calluses touching him everywhere.

"Thank you, honey." Mackey's head fell forward at his touch. "That's good."

He thought so too. He went quiet and concentrated on what he was doing, suddenly noticing all the scars. It was like they hadn't been there before; he hadn't even registered the ones up here until now. But they were everywhere, big and small; some were nothing really, but some of them were pretty deep. He touched one wide as his finger and traced it. "Wow. I bet this hurt."

"It did. Got stepped on in the chute. Burned like a bitch." Mackey moved to where he could rub easier.

"Do you mind me touching them? I should have asked..."

"No. They're not going anywhere, and I ain't ashamed."

"Nothing to be ashamed of. You earned them." Now that he could reach, Sid got both hands on Mackey's shoulders and worked his thumbs into the muscle, careful not to go too hard. He had no idea what hurt and what didn't.

That made him grin. He should probably go on the assumption that everything did. Like, everything. Mackey's pinky toe probably hurt right now.

"Oh..." That sound was beyond sex, beyond anything as normal and good as orgasm.

"Oh yeah?" Sid chuckled and kept it up. "Does sports medicine travel with a massage therapist? They should. You could really use one."

"Nah. It's one hell of an idea, though." Mackey's words were soft, fuzzy. That was sweet as anything.

He felt himself breathing deeper, enjoying the feel of the warm damp skin under his fingers. His touch was curious, working muscle but also carving long trails and tracing scars. "It's been a long time since I--"

Touched anyone. Really touched them. But he couldn't say that. *Jesus. Think.* "Felt this relaxed."

Better. Or at least safer.

"You got good hands." Mackey looked up at him with those gorgeous eyes. "Real good."

"Thanks." He ran a hand over the top of Mackey's head, rubbing the bright blond crew cut. "You ready to turn in cowboy? It's been a long day."

"I am. I'm trying to convince myself not to just sleep right here. I'm melted."

Sid laughed. "You'll get pruney. That's not pretty."

"True that. Come upstairs, and we'll sleep hard." Mackey

turned and took his hand, kissed his knuckles in a motion old as time. "Thanks for road tripping with me, honey."

Then Mackey headed for the stairs.

"You're...welcome." He stared at his hand, brought the place Mackey had kissed up to his own lips thoughtfully. Mixed signals from the cowboy. Not like his were clear, he supposed; they weren't even clear to himself.

Mackey hauled himself up, dragging his feet up the stairs with a soft sigh.

"The road trip was fun, but I appreciate having somewhere to road trip to." His brother, the golden boy, had thrown a wrench in his plans. But this was good. This was an adventure.

"Oh, I can't wait for you to see the house. It's a hoot and a half. I got me plans." Mackey wrapped the towel around his waist.

"I want to hear all about them." He hung his towel over his shoulders and picked up their beer bottles. "I'm dying to see the place."

"Yeah? Cool. It's big and old and weird and possibly haunted." Mackey chuckled softly. "Like a ghost would dare live with a cowboy."

He looked at Mackey curiously as they made their way toward the elevators. "Ghosts don't like cowboys?"

"Not bull fighters. We're fierce." Mackey led the way back to the room. When they got there, the beds had been turned down, and there were two huge pieces of chocolate cake waiting.

"Oh, dude. Cake! It's good to be your roommate." He started to dive right for it but remembered his manners at the last minute. Likely too late to save face so he made a show of it, hiding his hands behind his back and walking past the tray. "After you."

"Oh, be my guest, honey. See if they left us ice cream in the little fridge? I do love ice cream."

He grinned and opened the little freezer. "Yep. Chocolate. Apparently they know you love ice cream too." Sid pulled it out and opened it, stuck a spoon in it, and held it out to Mackey.

"You want to share it on your cake? I'll split it with you." Mackey dropped the towel and grabbed his sweats.

"Thanks, but would you believe I don't care for chocolate ice cream?" He turned his back and dug through his bag for his PJs. "Love chocolate, just not in ice cream."

"No shit? I love all ice creams, I think." Mackey sat on the edge of one of the beds, pulling on a pair of loose knit pants with…

"Are those flaming armadillos?"

"Yeah, fan made 'em for me."

"Man, you get all the cool things." Sid laughed, then shucked his trunks and pulled on his PJs bottoms in record time, trying not to blush. "Cake time."

"Sounds about right. Damn, it smells good." Mackey settled on the bed with ice cream and cake. "Let's see if I can make a dent in this."

Sid sat on the side of the other bed and tucked his feet up under him. "Just smoosh it with your fork and you'll be good." He took a big bite, and it was sweet and rich and perfect. "Oh, mmm. Fuck yeah."

Mackey watched him, just long enough that he'd just started to notice, when the cowboy took a bite of his own.

"Good cake." Yeah, okay. That was embarrassing. And… nice, too.

"It is. Feel free to take another bite. That was great." Mackey winked, playing with him, not a hint of meanness in those eyes.

"You liked that, huh?" He tried to play along. "Do they do their own baking here, do you know?" That wasn't a real question, that was an excuse for Mackey to keep looking. He took another bite, and hammed it up a little, enjoying it like he had the first one. "Mhm... so good."

"I think there's a bakery here that does their cakes." Mackey ate mainly the ice cream, eyes never leaving Sid's mouth.

"Cool." Very cool. That signal was a little less mixed. Sid stretched his legs out and rested his back against the headboard. "Man. This is a long morning at the gym right here. It'll be worth it though." He glanced over at Mackey again. "How's the ice cream?"

"Good. Rich, cold -- I'm a fan."

He tossed the remote over. "I picked last night." He wasn't going to fall right asleep with all this sugar in his system. He should probably get a shower and get the chlorine off too.

"I'll find something. Something not rodeo, right?" Mackey's laugh was so fine, so low.

"Something not rodeo, thank you. Unless you find a rebroadcast of some brilliant set of takes I did, then you know, we can talk." He gave Mackie a sideways grin. "It's a rare but beautiful thing."

"Your brilliance?" Mackey turned on some random infomercial and turned down the volume.

"Yeah. That." He snorted and took another bite of chocolate sin.

"Shit, I can't do what you do. Couldn't even begin to imagine how. I just got to keep three guys working and fifty guys alive."

He glanced up at Mackey's words, finding not a hint of guile in the expression.

"Oh." He stared at Mackey. "That's all?" He couldn't help the sarcasm. "Well, fuck. Why isn't everyone doing it?"

"Not everyone's meant to take a hit like we are. I think it's genetic."

"I was joking, man. Nobody can do what you do. Not like you do it. Not with that much heart. You... you and the team? You're like... unstoppable. A force of nature."

"You should have met the team ten years ago when I was just a babe." Mackey's expression went distant and fond. "Clay, Puddin', Davy -- they were magic."

One of the things he had learned? Ten years was the difference between a baby and an old man in the rodeo business.

Everyone knew his heroes. They were in books, in the music he listened to, in his family. He had no idea who these guys were Mackey was talking about, but he was going to find out. "Tell me about them. Like, what sort of guy goes by 'Puddin''?"

"Oh, lord have mercy. Puddin' is a big ole boy from South Carolina that blew out his knees bulldogging. He's a funny man, light on his feet. Retired after Clay died and has eight little girls now. Him and Tommy? Shit, man, you talk about fighting? Those two tied it up daily."

That sounded like Tommy. He hadn't seen it himself, but he could tell the Aussie had an eye for trouble. "You'd think they'd be happy with the bruises they got on the dirt."

"You'd think, but Puddin', he was old school, and my Tommy, well, he's not. Me, I'm stuck in the middle, mostly. Well, I mean, I guess I'm the old school now, and Tommy's in the middle."

His Tommy. Mackey was loyal. If loyal was old school, count him in. "I'm usually not old school, but the more I hang out with you the more I wonder." Sid winked at him and got up to set the rest of his cake in the fridge. It would go great with coffee in the morning.

"You mind putting mine in too, honey. The ice cream was enough." Mackey murmured his thanks as he took the plate. "Davy went back to California when he retired, lives on the beach, happy as a pig in shit. Tommy took Davy's spot in the team, and finally I wasn't the low man on the totem pole."

He closed the fridge and stretched out on his bed propped up on an elbow. "I am having a hard time imagining you as low man anywhere."

"No? It was a thing. I been doing this for, what? Fifteen years as a pro, been head bull fighter for damn near six. So I spent five years as the gopher, and the one that slept in the back of the truck with the dogs when the hotel was full up."

"You don't do that to the twins, so... maybe not as old school as you think. Where did you find them?"

"They come from rodeo folks -- momma and granny were racers, daddy and both their older brothers are ropers. Their folks trusted me to keep them." Mackey chuckled softly. "Figured they were safer with me than on their own."

That made him laugh. "That's saying something, huh?"

"Those boys are a disaster, but as good as the day is long. Good bull fighters too. Not interested in politics or drama."

"I'm not either, but somehow I end up in it. I think it might be unavoidable for me." Sid yawned and stretched out on his back. He was tired. Good tired, but ready to get some sleep. He hit the light by the bed, leaving Mackey the light from the infomercial. "I'm figuring it out though--who to talk to about what, who not to. Who to trust implicitly and who to completely avoid."

"You're a smart kid, honey. I ain't worried about you." Mackey grabbed his phone and earphones. "Sleep well."

"I'm not a kid." He chuckled. "So not a kid."

"Yeah, thank God for that." The TV went off, and Mackey's phone light came on, the man obviously used to sharing a room.

"Take your meds. And don't stay up too late." He yawned again and closed his eyes. "Night, Mackey."

"Night, honey. Sleep well."

16

They pulled up to the house late -- around nine thirty, damn near ten -- and it was a welcome sight to have the kitchen light on. Better than that, the entire roof was lined with big, bright Christmas lights.

"Look at that!" It wasn't home yet, but it was getting better every time. "I had Vicki leave the light on, but she didn't tell me her boys had put Christmas lights up. She said she stocked the fridge and made muffins." She came in twice a month to flush toilets and dust, clear the fridge. That shit.

Mackey hadn't bothered with the pain pills last night, but tonight he was thinking he ought. Everything hurt. Everything.

Still, they were home.

"Vicki?" Sid shut the truck off and stretched, and he heard Sid's back pop. "Oh man. That felt good."

"Little lady that I pay to clean. Her husband and boys fix fence and roofs and shit. They cleared the road for us." They were the ones who'd taught him about bears.

He had a momma bear on his land. Damn, that rocked his world.

The house was a big old thing -- all windows and pine. It was going to be something one day. It was going to sparkle.

"Oh, that's handy that you have them." Sid slid out of the truck with a groan. The man had obviously had enough of driving. "Beautiful night. Look at all the stars. I'll grab the bags."

"Yeah. I'm coming." He took his go bag and his gear. He was fixin' to have to do a shit-ton of laundry. "Come on in. I'll give you the tour."

"Tell me I get a tour of the outside when it's daylight. What an amazing place. The views from all those windows must be incredible." Sid craned his neck to look up at the second floor. "And the lights... so neat. Festive. It actually feels kind of like Christmas now."

"They surprised me with those." He took the stairs slow, rubbing the belly of the bear carved into the column, and then put in the code for the front door. "Come on in."

The house smelled like sap and vanilla and leather, and he flipped a switch, letting the lights fill the front room. "Kitchen's behind you. You got your choice of rooms -- the master is upstairs, and there's one guest room down here that's all made up."

"I'll do the guest then. If it's easy. Thank you." Sid walked into the room and wandered, looking impressed. "So much woodwork, so no wonder it's taking forever to fix up. But it's beautiful. It will be gorgeous when it's done. Wow."

"Thank you. It's--" Going to be home someday. He hoped. "--All mine."

"I'm a little jealous. I own nothing. I don't even own a car." Sid dumped his bag at the foot of the stairs. "Tour first? Or are you hungry?"

"Come on, tour first." They'd been snacking all day, after all. "There are six bedrooms -- or so they told me. There's four rooms filled with old crap. I have two cleaned out. There's a guest house too, but I haven't even started on that." He shot the kid a grin. "The good news is five out of seven bathrooms are functional."

The big master bath wasn't working yet, because he was going to make the whole upper floor a great big suite for him.

"Well gosh, I can take a dump in a different bathroom every day of the week." Sid nodded seriously and then broke out in giggles.

"If you can find it, you can shit." He almost -- almost -- kept a straight face. "Come on, butthead. Leave your bag, we'll start upstairs. My bed's there, but I'm intending to totally redo it. I want it to be one massive suite."

"When I grow up I want to be someone who can say that." Sid grinned and followed him upstairs. "No, I don't mean the butthead part, butthead."

"Oh, damn. You can leave your bag anytime." Sid sure didn't seem to mind the flirting, and there was something about the kid. Something damn kind. He approved.

At the top of the stairs, Sid went right for one of the windows. "Oh wow. The moon just lights everything up out here, huh? Look at that. The view must be pretty good from here I guess."

"It is. Come out on the balcony. It stretches all the way across the house." He opened the door, the moonlight pouring in.

Sid slipped out the door like the moon was pulling on him and went right to the railing, slowly walking the length of it, eyes roaming the distance as he tucked his coat tighter. "Mackey, this is gorgeous. Look at how the moon lights up the snow, the trees. I've never seen anything like that."

"It's a wonderland, ain't it? You can ski right out, they said." He hadn't tried, but he intended to learn.

"Yeah? Cool. I'm terrible but I love it. I also don't own skis, so that could be a thing." Sid laughed and leaned on the railing.

"I don't either, but I guess I will. Sooner rather than later." He rolled up on his toes, stretching some, his muscles creaking at him. "I got elk, deer, there's a momma bear out here on the back acreage. She's sleeping hard now, I bet."

"I have a dumpster and a couple of homeless guys behind my building." Sid's eyes crinkled playfully. "Not quite as glamorous but pretty damn wild."

"I never lived in an apartment. That's pretty different. I worked bull ridings in New York City, though. It's something else." He couldn't imagine living there, but all that meant was that he didn't imagine real well.

"I'm thinking about going up there after the holidays sometime... if you're interested. Bring anybody you want. I'll show you around." Sid pushed off the railing and wandered farther along the balcony.

"Sure. I'd like that." He didn't follow, because he didn't want the kid to feel trapped. He was happy to just flirt and play.

"Cool. I'm working on a place to stay. Could even be my place if my subletter is out of town." Sid stopped, crossed the balcony to a window, and looked in. "Master Bedroom?"

"Yeah, go on in." It ought to be decent. The sheets were clean.

The doors opened into a huge master, the wood beams heavy along the slope of the ceiling.

"Oh wow." Sid walked right into the middle of the room

and turned in a slow circle. "I love all the wood details in this house. And the exposed beams. So cool. And you're opening up this whole floor?"

"That's my plan, yeah. I want to make a big old huge master and master bath -- walk in shower, sauna, jacuzzi, all of it."

"You need a big bed. Like a tall one, with wooden posts, you know? Thick, carved posts. Something heavy and masculine." Sid stood at the foot of his bed and nodded. "That would be hot."

"Yeah? I can see that. I just had the mattress delivered, but yeah, yeah, I like that idea." Oh, he could imagine that, no problem.

"Right?" Sid looked at him sidelong. "Sleep like royalty in your master suite."

"I figure, once I retire, I'll be here all the time. I ought to make it yummy." Yummy, that was a technical term.

Sid took a couple of steps closer, grinning. "Hell, if I had all of this I'd retire tomorrow."

"Yeah? One day. One day I'll be done with my work." And one day this place would feel like home.

Sid's head tilted thoughtfully. "One day. I guess so."

"What about you? What do you want to do, once you're not doing this no more?" What was Sid's dream?

Sid shrugged. "I have no idea. I didn't see this coming, so I doubt I'll see whatever that is until I get there. I'm sure it'll be good, whatever it is."

He nodded. He liked that. It was the way things tended to work. The good Lord gave you what all He reckoned you needed.

Sid nodded back like he knew they understood each other. "Show me more."

"You got it." He showed off the not-working yet en suite,

the not-decent yet bonus room up here, and the bathroom that worked, then took him back down the stairs.

"Which project are you going to focus on this—whoa—" Sid tripped behind Mackey, missing the last step and falling into him, but righting himself quickly. "Sorry about that." Was that hand on his ass on purpose? If it was, it didn't last long. Sid stepped around him. "I'm just going to grab my bag."

"I'll show you to your room. It's all put together nice." It was the rodeo room, from silver buckles to chaps to wallpaper made of programs. He loved it.

"Sure. Great." Sid followed him in and tossed his bag up on the bed. "Oh, look. Rodeo!" Sid laughed, teasing. "I'm kidding. This is your whole life. I was wondering where you kept this stuff. Look at this wallpaper. Wow. You've spent a little time working in here, huh?"

Sid wandered, stopping to get a good look at the buckles. "These are really neat."

He stepped right up, letting himself get close enough to feel Sid's heat. "Those are all mine, from different events, finals. I'm honored to have so many to show."

Sid took a deep breath, shoulders leaning toward Mackey as his chest filled. "Impressive."

He let Sid rest against him, feeling a body that was so much more solid than it seemed in the suits. Lord, Sid was fine, and his hand came to rest on the lean waist.

"No one has ever kissed my hand before." Sid took his hand and held it for a second, then slid it around to rest against hard abs. He could feel Sid's heartbeat, strong against his ribs.

"No?" He let his thumb explore, stroking and petting, while the rest of his hand stayed still. "That's a shame. You deserve to be...respected."

"I do." Sid laughed softly. "As do you, though I don't know that I'd call what I've been thinking about you respectful."

"No? I can get...behind that." Oh, he was funny. Really. He made himself smile.

"I can't decide if we're fighting this or both waiting for the other to make a move. And either way, I can't figure out why. I mean, you didn't make a move on the balcony in the moonlight? What's the matter with you?" He got another laugh, but Sid still didn't turn around.

"I got to admit, honey. I'm usually way drunker when things get hot and heavy the first time." Sid was different. He wasn't sure why, but he reckoned that didn't matter. "And I wasn't sure how bad a turn off the stitches might be."

Sid did turn then and ran a thumb across his cheek. "Your eyes shine so bright I can't even see them."

Mackey blinked, and he swore to God that his heart stopped. No one'd ever -- ever -- said nothing like that to him. Not ever, and he wasn't sure he could remember how to breathe.

"There's more here than hot and heavy." Sid kissed his cheek softly. Everything Sid did was so gentle. "Though there's plenty of that too."

"Yeah. I'm interested in both." He wrapped his hand around Sid's hip, loving the way the man fit.

The look in Sid's eyes went from sweet to smoldering just like that. "I don't know what being with a rodeo cowboy means really, but I'm ready to find out."

"You want to bring your bag upstairs, honey?" He wasn't going to fuck with a man he wouldn't sleep with.

Sid looked at him, eyes searching his. "Have you ever been on a date?"

"A date? Not since my momma made me take Charlene

Kay to prom when I was fifteen." She'd been pregnant and upset, and Momma had given him fifty bucks to take her.

"Have you ever... just held hands?" Sid threaded their fingers together. "Just made out with someone? Just snuggled and watched TV?"

Ah, he'd pushed too hard. Never let it be said he was an asshole. He didn't want Sid to think that at all. "I'm real good at sitting and leaning hard. Real good. Hell, I got a TV here in the den dealie." He tugged Sid's hand, wanting to get out of the bedroom so that he didn't feel nasty. "Come on, honey. I still got that to show you, plus the back deck."

"Did I hurt your feelings?" Sid tugged back, not moving. "I didn't mean to. I'm just trying to get to know you. All those things I was asking about, they're things I think you deserve, that's all."

"You're a good man." He wasn't used to dealing with guys that wanted to spend time and get busy. Jack, really. But Jack was just mostly a good friend that would give a guy a hand.

"You are too." Sid let go of him and shouldered his bag. "Still want me to take this upstairs?"

"I do. I mean, I don't want you to feel...pressured or nothing. I'd hate you to think I was a dick." He grinned at Sid. "I was fixin' to say I wasn't nasty, but...well, I ain't an angel in bed, so..."

Sid's eyes narrowed. "The first time I jacked off with you on my mind I was thinking about the look in your eyes when you were trying not to hit me." One of Sid's eyebrows climbed up, and he grinned, then turned and headed for the stairs.

"Oh ho. You want coffee, honey?" he called after that fine, fine retreating ass.

"Yes. With Bailey's in it, if you have it." Sid trotted up the stairs and disappeared.

Well, damn. He could manage that. He so could.

He shook his head as he meandered to the kitchen. Lord, he hoped the stitches didn't pull too bad, because he did like kissing.

17

Sid dumped his bag down at the foot of the bed and looked around Mackey's bedroom. He shook his head at himself, his grin turning into a chuckle, and then becoming an outright laugh.

Jesus Christ. He'd just roped in a rodeo cowboy.

Now to see if it would last more than eight seconds.

He didn't know what the hell he thought he was doing. They worked together. Or not even really; they were corporate and cowboy, and everyone, even Danny, said the two didn't mix well. He'd been at that dinner with Brad and Cody. He'd seen it himself.

And if this didn't work out…

Well, they kind of rumbled at each other on a professional level anyway, right? Maybe it wasn't worth worrying about. Yet.

He knew that made no sense. That eventually they were going to have to deal with all of that like grownups. But that was the story he was going with for now because fuck, he wanted Mackey.

Bad.

He wanted all those other things he'd talked about too, and he was going to make sure Mackey got them. But there was a powerful energy building between them, and they needed to get the edge off before he could think about romance. They had a couple weeks; they had time.

Okay that was decided. Sid hadn't seen this job coming, hadn't seen Mack coming—*yet, haha*—so he wasn't going to worry about whatever came next. He took another look around and headed back downstairs.

A cheery whistle filled the air, the smell of coffee strong and welcome. This place was huge, and Mackey acted like he didn't quite know what to do about all the space, but in the kitchen, the man seemed totally at home.

"Oh, that smells good." Now that things were clearer, he wasn't going to tiptoe around and confuse the cowboy. He went right to Mackey and put an arm around his waist. "Just what the doctor ordered."

"Coffee and Baileys is important. Especially when it gets real cold."

Like it wasn't damned frigid right now. It had to be in the teens at least.

"This isn't Christmas in New York, that's for sure. I thought it was cold *there* this time of year." He looked around. They needed... "Music?"

"Tell Alexa what you want, honey. She'll play anything."

He looked around and found the device on the counter. "Schmancy. Alexa, play Christmas music." And just like that, the kitchen filled with the Temptations, trumpets, and jingle bells. He did a little shimmy with his shoulders to the beat of the music. "Cool."

"Yeah, I have another one upstairs so that I can listen to it when I fall asleep."

"Oh good. I like music in the bedroom. And you don't

have neighbors to worry about like I do in New York, so we can crank it up." Sid liked that idea, a lot.

"Yeah?" Mackey handed him his coffee, then leaned on the Saltillo tile countertop. "I been in hotel rooms forever, so I can't sleep with quiet. And here? It's *damn* quiet."

"I'm not quiet." Sid sipped his coffee. "God, I'm so glad not to be in a hotel tonight."

"Well, we got a good long time to take it easy." That was a satisfied sound Mackey made, wasn't it? "I need to get me a Christmas tree, don't I?"

"You do. Lights, ornaments, and we could have some fun decorating. I haven't put up a tree in forever. And we've got twelve whole days before Christmas." It sounded fantastic. "We can get up to a lot in twelve days."

"Yessir." Oh, look at that smile -- slow and lazy, but somehow filthy and wonderful.

"We'll make some noise." Sid gave Mackey a look and leaned closer, flirting. "Maybe finish the demolition of that master bath?"

"Oh now, you do know the way to a man's heart. Laying tile? Sexy." Oh, Mackey was good at this. Excellent.

"Hey. I'm really good with the...the what's it." Oh damn. "Glue... stuff." He gave Mackey a sheepish look, trying not to laugh. "No. No, I'm really not."

Mackey's laughter rang out, filling the space and warming it immediately, chasing the shadows from the corners of the ceilings.

"I don't know what I was trying to--oh! Grout!" He cracked up. "That could have sounded dirty if I'd pulled it off. Right? Maybe?" The giggles wouldn't let up, so he put his coffee down before he spilled it.

"As in, oh! Grout my cracks, bay-bee! Grout it all!"

Okay, Mackey might kill him. He blushed hard. He

could feel his cheeks burning. "Jesus Christ. That's the least sexy sounding thing ever."

"Honey, laying tile is not sexy. Satisfying? Sure. Sexy? Fuck no."

He chuckled, finally able to breathe a little. "I love your laugh. It's so open and real."

"Folks have fake laughs a lot, you think?"

"Well, I don't know. I think so. I think some people grow up and forget what real joy feels like. But when you laugh, that's what it sounds like."

Mackey blushed a pretty, bright rose. "Well, thank you, sir."

"You're welcome. Just the truth." He shrugged and took a sip of his coffee, then set it down again. "The Eagles. Dance with me?"

"Sure. I...Show me how?"

Wait. Mackey didn't know how? Sid wanted to ask how a guy grew up anywhere and did not know how to dance, but he didn't want to embarrass the cowboy.

"Sure." He took Mackey's coffee and set it down. "So, left hand on my shoulder, right hand in my left...yeah, like that." He slid his right hand around Mackey's back, fingers resting firmly under one shoulder blade. "Okay? Just relax and let me lead."

It took Mackey a few steps, but he could tell the man was used to moving with a team, responding to cues. Soon Mackey was dancing with him, easy, like they'd been doing it for hours.

"You've got it. Man, is there anything you can't do? Okay, try this." Sid turned Mackey in a circle and really shouldn't have been surprised at the way Mackey moved. "Good. Now we just... enjoy it."

"That's the easy part." Mackey winked at him, relaxed

and easy in his torn and bruised skin. "You're good at this."

"My mother taught me. We'd dance all the time. She loved to, and Dad really isn't the dancing type." In the kitchen while dinner was cooking, on the back deck in the summer, the living room on a cold night in winter... she was always dancing. "It came in handy when she made me take Kaitlyn to the prom senior year... sound familiar? Moms are funny like that, huh?"

"They are. Your folks still around? Y'all close?"

"Dad's in Pennsylvania. Mom died three years ago... little more now." He tucked his arm tighter around Mackey, drawing them closer.

"I'm sorry, honey." Mackey kissed the corner of his lips, then his jaw, the touch feather-light and gentle as fuck, making him hum with pleasure.

"Shit happens. You can keep doing that, though. That's nice." He didn't want sympathy; he was still angry. He felt like he might always be. Someday they'd tell each other all about how they'd each lost their parents. He was thinking it should involve more than coffee and Bailey's.

"I can. I'm good at it, even." Mackey managed to drop kisses all over his jaw and chin without ever kissing him full on.

"Mmm. You are." Sid turned his head suddenly and caught Mackey's lips with his. The dancing stopped as he slipped one hand into the cowboy's hair, encouraging Mackey to stay there.

Mackey hummed softly, and the kiss slowly -- like millimeter by millimeter -- deepened. Mackey tasted him, tongue teasing his lips open, dipping inside.

He opened farther and met Mackey's tongue with his own, and the warm, easy vibe too. So curious that the toughest man on earth had such tenderness in him, but Sid wasn't really surprised. He'd already seen Mackey about as vulnerable as a man could get the night of that horrid migraine. His spine tingled, knowing that they had this and a lot more to explore together.

Mackey's hand meandered around to the small of his back, finding the sensitive spot like the man knew it was there, fingertips dragging above his belt and playing him.

"Mmm." He started to sway with Mackey, letting the music back in. Sid was used to guys that worked at smelling great--aftershave and cologne, fine leather and the city. Mackey smelled like the earth, like the air, musky and all man. Sid had never been this close to anyone like him.

He felt Mackey's stitches scrape his chin and was reminded that the cowboy was still hurting. He leaned back just enough to catch those amazing blue eyes. "You good? You want to get off your feet?"

"I'm right as rain, honey. Ain't never been asked to dance before."

"This won't be the last time. You took right to it. There really isn't a better excuse to hold someone, especially in--" Hm. He was going to say *in public* but...probably not. That was something he hadn't thought about, and he wasn't going to right now. They weren't. "Well there isn't one."

"Yeah. I can think of a couple, but most of 'em are better naked." Mackey patted his ass, squeezed.

"We'll get there. Right now we're dancing in your kitchen, and I'm just getting a feel for all this muscle." Sid gripped Mackey's biceps and gave them a squeeze. He was in pretty good shape but what Mackey had going on no one could get at the gym. The man was made of pure stone, no fat, no give, all muscle.

Sid tugged Mackey's T-shirt out of the front of his jeans and caught the man's eyes again before sliding one hand underneath to rest against Mackey's warm skin. Fuck, feel that -- those muscles rippled and rolled, dancing under his fingers like they had minds of their own.

"I wanted to touch you so bad at the pool last night. Your hand around my ankle was totally chill, but it might as well have been foreplay. No lie."

"I was afraid you'd think I was a dirty old man, but you were right there. So pretty."

"Dirty? Maybe. Not that I mind one bit." Sid laughed, spreading out his fingers and sliding them over Mackey's skin. "Old? Are you kidding?"

"Ancient." Mackey groaned and took another kiss, this one tinged with need, pushing a little harder.

There you are.

Sid was so ready for this. He hummed into the kiss, adding his other hand under the T-shirt and pulling it loose. He slid his hands higher, thumbs gliding over nipples that hardened at the touch. Oh, that made Mackey groan and drag him in tighter, need pushing into his thigh.

He pushed back, making sure Mackey knew he wasn't the only one feeling it. Sid reached back and tugged his own sweater off over his head, then shoved purposefully at the flannel Mackey had on over his T-shirt. "Want your skin."

Mackey nodded, but those eyes were focused on him, running from his crotch up to his eyes, then back. "Damn, you're fine to me."

Then Mackey shrugged off his flannel before oh-so carefully pulling the neckline of his t-shirt out, stretching it to get it over his head without pulling the stitches.

"You... you're... just so fucking hot." They were very different though. Mackey was scarred and seemed to have a permanent tan, and Sid felt like he looked like he'd been brought up in a tower by comparison. City-pale, smooth, and the only real scar he had was from when he'd had his appendix out in college.

"And you make me dizzy. I could eat you up." Mackey put his hands in the center of his belly, then slid them up, never once losing connection.

"Works for m-me... oh." His abs clenched under the touch and the next breath he took trembled with it; he couldn't quite get enough air.

"I do like the way you smell, honey." Mackey took a deep breath, nostrils flaring.

Jesus, he'd swear that was the hottest thing he'd ever seen. He arched, grinding against Mackey, cock going hungry and hard so fast it made him lightheaded. "Mackey."

"Yeah, honey." Mackey nodded for him, then spun him so that fuzzy chest was against his back, letting him see himself in the glass door. Mackey cupped his cock, thumb sliding along his length. "Let me touch you?"

Fuck, yes. He nodded when no words came out and swallowed hard. "Please."

Mackey unfastened his jeans, fishing out his cock with a confident hand, never once looking away from him. "You're so damn pretty."

Then Mackey's calloused fingers started working him, up and down, base to tip.

Sid hissed and leaned back, looping a hand up behind Mackey's neck for balance. "You've done this a few times before, huh?" The touch was perfect. Strong and sure. He watched their reflection in the glass, fascinated by the way Mackey moved, and how the bull fighter's shoulders stretched wider than his own.

"I love the way a man's cock feels in my hand, honey, and yours is a work of art."

Sure. They all kind of were, right? But he'd take it.

"Thank you." He pressed his hips back, ass rubbing nicely into Mackey's groin. "Mmm. I feel you."

"Good." On the next upstroke, Mackey rolled his palm over the tip, electricity shooting through him.

"Oh. God." The part of him that was always trying to run things wanted him to stop Mackey, move them out of the kitchen to the bedroom where this kind of behavior was appropriate. Without that impulsive piece of himself he literally would not be in Mackey's kitchen, so he pushed it aside and let himself feel, giving not one fuck about what was appropriate. It felt way too good to deny.

It was Mackey's show right now, and he was going to let the man have anything he wanted. He gasped and his thighs started to tremble, need and heat taking over the last bit of rational thought. He was happy to see it go.

"So fucking fine," Mackey growled, keeping up the assault on his senses, that hand never stopping, the rhythm steady and sure.

"Mackey?" There were questions in that name he couldn't find words for and need he couldn't refuse. His free hand flailed, finally finding the seam down the side of Mackey's jeans and holding on tight. "Fuck!" Sid let Mackey have his weight as he shot hard, fracturing into a million tiny pieces.

When he floated back down to earth, Mackey was holding his cock, just giving him pressure and heat, the hand steady and sure.

"That...fuck." He found his feet and turned around, offering a kiss, fingers going for Mackey's belt. "Now you."

"Come sit on the sofa with me? I want you so bad I ache, balls to bones."

"Sure." He buttoned up so he didn't trip over his jeans

and followed, one hand in Mackey's. "Wherever you want. Would you rather head upstairs?"

"Sure. I got a nice bed. Room for us to get comfy." Mackey headed for the stairs. "Alexa, turn off the kitchen lights and lock up."

"Your house locks itself up?" Sid chuckled, still breathless as he followed close.

"It does. I love it. It's like magic." Mackey shot him this wild grin, young and excited as hell.

"It's totally magic. Have you tried asking her to blow you?" Sid giggled his way up the steps.

Mackie snorted. "That has not crossed my mind, honey, but thank you for the thought."

"I'm totally fascinated by a magic lady locking your doors for you."

"I had the twins set this whole thing up. To me it might as well be Santa Claus."

Which would make sense, except he'd seen Mackey make that iPhone squeal in the truck. This wasn't a technophobe.

"Uh-huh. You're not as dumb as you like people to think you are." Sid took Mackey by the belt and dragged him over to the bed.

"No?" Mackey's prick was hard as a rock, leaking and leaving a wet spot on his jeans. "You sure?"

"Very sure. But it works for you, so I won't tell." He tugged and unzipped and wiggled until Mackey's jeans slid down and that proud cock popped right into his hand.

Mackey made a little strangled sound, and then rolled up right into his touch. "Damn honey."

Mackey's cock was heavy in his fingers, the skin like hot silk as he slid them down to the tip. He drew his thumb around and then pressed it firmly through the slippery cleft in the head, eyes flicking up to Mackey's to see how it felt.

Those blue eyes were like lasers, staring at him, burning in his skull. "Again."

He didn't shy away, returning the stare as he circled and then pushed his thumb through again. Then he stroked down to the root and back before he did it a third time. "Good?"

"Uhn."

Sid was fairly sure that was a good thing. Seriously.

"Uh-huh. You like that, you're going to love my tongue." He gave Mackey a little shove onto the bed, dropped to his knees, and tugged Mackey's jeans down farther. Mackey wiggled for him, moving enough that they could work together to get the man's jeans off. Every place he touched, he found scars, some tiny, some ropy and thick, most irregular, but a few that were obviously a surgeon's work.

"I have lots of exploring to do here." Sid traced one or two but didn't linger; he didn't want to try Mackey's patience. Instead he pushed Mackey's knees wide and moved in between thighs of pure muscle and nuzzled into the bull fighter's hip, inhaling deeply. "Mmm. Fuck you smell good." Wild. Dark. Hot as fuck cowboy.

"Make a man insane, swear to God." He loved that need in Mackey's voice.

"Just getting started." He took Mackey in hand again and stroked slowly, catching the man's eyes. "Beautiful cock, tough guy. I want a taste."

"Fuck, yes. Please." Mackey was into him, into this, and those eyes were burning down at him.

Sid slid his fingers up to the ridge at the head, keeping his eyes on Mackey as he painted the tip with a flat tongue.

Mackey blew out a heavy breath, like he was one of the bulls, the sound ridiculously hot, pure sex.

He was the luckiest man on earth.

He grinned and winked at Mackey, looked down, and concentrated on driving the cowboy out of his mind, starting with keeping his promise. He did one more circle and then drove his tongue through the little ravine deep enough to taste bitter salt.

Mackey bit out a curse word, and the rough, square hands tangled in the sheets.

That was beautiful. Sid wrapped his lips over the head and stroked Mackey with a firm hand, but this time he teased, touching and stroking the tip with light flicks of his tongue.

He could read Mackey's pleasure in the ripples of the taut abs, in the husky cries.

God, he wanted to make the cowboy howl. He wanted to make the man lose control, to totally own something so wild, even if it was just for a minute.

He took one more trip through Mackey's leaking slit, pressing hard and deep with the tip of his tongue, then dove in, taking Mackey's deep into his throat.

"Fuck!" Mackey's hand found his shoulder, the grip hard, not shy at all.

Encouraged, he drew up until he could circle and dive in with his tongue again, then swallowed Mackey down, throat working. He kept up the pattern, relentless, pushing Mackey toward the finish line.

Mackey's entire body was hard as stone, the muscles standing out in stark relief as he shook and moaned. There was a low, needy sound, and then Mackey squeezed as that heavy prick parted his lips the slightest bit more.

Fuck yeah, come on. Electricity shot up Sid's spine and he closed his eyes, letting Mackey take what he needed.

Mackey fucked his lips, desperate deep thrusts, then Sid heard a wild cry as spunk filled his mouth.

"Mmm." Hell yes. Sid sucked and licked Mackey lazily, finding the spots that made him shiver, catching his gaze again and keeping the cowboy sensitive as long as possible. Then he nuzzled into one thigh and sighed.

"D-damn, honey. You...damn. That was fucking beautiful."

He chuckled softly and got to his feet, reaching for the covers to pull them down. "I try." He climbed into bed and held a hand out. "Come on, tough guy. Climb in here with me."

"God yes. So glad you're here." Mackey slipped into bed and, to his surprise, cuddled right in.

"Me too. I didn't see this coming either." He tucked Mackey in close. "I still can hardly believe it."

"Mmhmm...in the morning, we'll have coffee on the balcony, turn on the heater out there. Maybe we'll see elk."

"Sounds perfect." He yawned hard but fought his eyes closing; he wanted to stay awake long enough for Mackey to fall asleep first.

Mackey stroked his belly, the caress gentle, soft, and it kept going, even after Mackey went heavy and quiet, breath evening out.

He tangled their fingers together. "Goodnight, Mackey."

18

Mackey woke up and slid out of the warm bed, tiptoeing around to put on his sweats and house shoes. He was wanting some Tylenol, some coffee, and a biscuit.

He could murder a biscuit.

He threw a half dozen frozen biscuits in the toaster oven and started the coffee brewing. Even with the sun shining, it was bitter out there, and there was a heavy lace of frost on the windows down here.

The biscuits were just coming out of the oven when he heard feet on the stairs. Sid appeared in the kitchen doorway in thick socks and a loosely tied robe. *His* robe, in fact.

"Good morning." Sid scrubbed a hand through his dark hair but that didn't help to straighten it. "I smelled something baking and fresh coffee and remembered I wasn't in a hotel."

"Biscuits. I was starving. Mornin', honey." God, that was just as cute as a button. Mackey could eat him up. "You want coffee?"

"Yes, please." Sid came to him and kissed his cheek. "Is it still snowing? It's chilly."

"Nope. It's still clear. Phone says we're in for another dumping in a couple days." Then they'd be in snow up to an elephant's ass.

"But we'll be all toasty in here with a fire in the fireplace and the heat on." Sid took the coffee he offered and sipped it. "Mmm. Nice. Can I have a biscuit?"

"Of course. I got some sausage, if you want, or there's butter and honey. I got no gravy, though." He wanted to bundle up with his breakfast and his new lover and sit on the balcony. The neat propane heater was another of his new toys. It was good to be him.

Sid must've had something similar on his mind and was hovering close. "What's easy?"

"Butter and honey?" It was easy, good, portable. All those words.

"Perfect. I want to go watch the sun on the snow. It looks like it's going to be a pretty day. Maybe we can bring some blankets out and snuggle."

"That's what I thought. I'm hoping to have a lovely, lazy morning." He got out the tub of butter and the honey bear, plus a knife. "I got paper plates."

Sid helped doctor up the biscuits while they were warm, and he topped off their coffees. "I think we're good. Bring on lazy." Sid's easy smile was warmer than his fancy new heaters would be.

"I've got a press up there full of blankets." They trundled upstairs balancing coffee and breakfast.

"Awesome. So, did you sleep okay?" Sid followed close behind and, when they got to the bedroom, peered out the doors that went to the balcony. "Shit, look at all the snow."

"I slept like the dead, thank you. It was amazing. You?"

He grabbed two puffy comforters. "There's a double swing out there that's stable and comfy. Let me turn out the outside heater."

"A swing and an outside heater? Whoa. I didn't see those last night." Sid did a quick change, pulling on sweats, a T-shirt and a heavy hoodie. "I slept great. I was with this hot cowboy last night that totally wrung me out."

"Yeah? I was wrapped around a hot little body that blew my mind, so that's fair." He had had a ball, playing with Sid. And there was something...easy about the man.

"We'll have to do it again sometime." Sid held the door with his back so Mackey could get out with the comforters. "I'm very open this holiday season."

"Promises." His eyes were fastened to that taut ass, and he could imagine sinking in and making Sid fly.

"I always keep them. Oh, how cool is that swing?"

"Isn't it?" He caught himself bouncing, like he did when he was fixin' to work. "I had it made. It's sturdy, cushy, and I love that Steve got the bears carved in."

"It's amazing. Come on, before you freeze." Sid set the food down on a little table, and they covered the swing with one of the comforters. "Let's bundle up while the coffee is still hot."

"Sounds perfect." They settled together, and Mackey got them covered up so the wind couldn't find its way in. The heater did its job, and Mackey understood that this -- this spot right here -- was going to be his favorite.

The fog was beginning to burn off down in the valley, and as the heavy mist eased back, dozens of huge, dark bodies appeared in the meadow in front of them. Elk. "Look, honey."

Sid gasped. "Whoa. Oh wow. Those are elk, right? I've never even seen *one*, let alone a whole herd..." Sid's spoke at barely above a whisper, but it was hard to say whether it was not to scare them off, or if he was just that awed. "Mackey, they're beautiful."

"Right? And so goddamn *big*." This was why he'd bought this huge old house that needed so much love. Because after thirty-some-odd weeks a year on the road, he needed this. He needed the mountains, he needed the stream running through his land, he needed the critters and the proof that the whole world wasn't concrete.

"I saw a moose once in New Hampshire. She was pretty damn big too. Long legs. But they don't travel in herds like this." Sid leaned into him. "No wonder you love this place. It's magical."

"It is. I love it. I can't wait until the house feels like home." He knew it would happen. He needed some time, some focus, some help, but it would happen.

"Let's work on it while we're here. Pick a project, and I'll help."

He blinked, then looked over at Sid. "Seriously?"

He didn't want Sid telling everyone he was mean, putting the man to work over Christmas.

Sid laughed, pretending to look shocked. "Yes, seriously. I've had coffee. I know what I'm offering. It'll be fun. And work. But mostly fun."

"I'd love some help. We can clean out the spare bedroom up here, that way the contractor can get to work." It was filled with boxes of god knew what.

"Sounds good." Sid held up a biscuit. "How long did you say you'd been here?"

"Five months, give or take. I closed on July fifteenth." He hadn't even been able to come up hardly until late August because he'd been busting his hump. Finally they'd all come up -- Tommy and the twins both -- and started into work.

"And you had your parents' place before that, right?" Sid curled warm fingers around his knee. "Have they been gone a long time?"

"Momma died about eight years ago from cancer, and Daddy lasted another three, but he never once lived again, you know? When his heart gave out, I'd been waiting for it. He didn't want to live without her. He always said she was his soul." And he'd loved them dearly, but losing Momma had hurt his heart, and he'd never felt like he could say so, because Daddy's pain had been so big. Who was he to cry over her?

"That sounds hard. Losing your mom is bad enough, but then watching that happen to your dad... that had to be rough."

"It wasn't fun. I think that's why I was happy to let the ranch go. All the joy had been sucked out of that land."

"It was a good move. This is a piece of heaven." Sid leaned forward, watching the herd of elk move as the sun glinted off the snow, and they disappeared into the trees.

"That was fucking cool, man. My own personal elk herd." He was so glad they'd been out to impress his new lover. It made him feel like a champ.

"You're like the wild animal whisperer. Bulls, elk..." Sid leaned into him again. "If I had a place like this, I'd never leave it."

"That's the plan one day. I need to have my place settled." He knew one day the right bull would make the wrong hit, and he'd be done. Then he'd come here, and he'd be happy.

"Hmm." Sid munched on a biscuit and talked around chewing. "A place like this... you'll be working on it forever.

You have to decide how done you need it to before you can move in."

"This is true. I know I need it cleaned up, and I have to get this floor done. I bet I live up here a lot." He imagined his bottom floor would be filled with cowboys, damn near all the time.

"It'll be amazing up here. Big bedroom, master bath, jacuzzi tub, sitting area… you could put speakers everywhere and fill the whole place with music." Sid grinned at him. "And that four-poster bed. Why leave?"

"Yeah. And there are snowmobiles, and I'm going to learn to ski, dammit. I want to explore." He had a bunch of plans, some important, some just fun.

"I can ski. Maybe not Colorado ski; the snow is all different out here. But I can Vermont ski. I've never been on a snowmobile though. We should try."

"Are they different? I mean, the skiing. Isn't it just skis and snow?" He knew there was cross country skiing and then fuck a doodle doo fast down the mountain type, but they had state-types too?

Sid chuckled. "I've been told there's a lot more loose, deep powder out here. Back east it's all packed powder and ice. You ski it differently. I think you even use different kinds of skis but don't quote me on that."

"No shit. Okay, now I'll have to keep you around. I had no idea. All the snow I've ever lived in is…well, the snow on the ground here, right now." He had so much to learn, and he was so excited about it. He wanted to see icicles.

"We get a fair amount every year. My brother and I used to be out in it all winter. Now that Dad's there alone mostly, it's less fun and more work."

Oh, poor baby. He was hoping that he wasn't bringing up bad thoughts. "Well, I'm sure in a few years, I'll be grumpy about it, but not yet. Now I'm looking forward to it."

"He complains, but I think that's mostly just to have something to complain about, you know?" Sid shrugged. "It can be a huge pain in the city, especially if there's a lot of it. The sidewalks get all slippery, and it piles up on the corner and doesn't stay white long. It's pretty neat when it's falling heavily though, the city gets so quiet."

"That's cool. You'll have to show me." They ended up that way a few times a year, and he wanted to see things that weren't on the 'humor the bull riders' tour.

"I will. I'll take you after the opening show. There may or may not be snow. After here, it'll seem balmy." Sid tucked a hand high up on his thigh. "At least I can guarantee tropical weather in the bedroom area."

"Mmm...I'm still a Texan at heart. I can handle the heat." He spread, just a little bit wider.

"I can handle watching you work up a sweat." Sid drained the last of his coffee and put the mug down.

"You've seen that before, but I'm totally into showing you again."

"I have, but not enough. Not nearly." Curious fingers ghosted over his prick, a light touch through the fabric of his sweats.

"No?" Oh fuck. How cool was this, knowing that they could do this, right out here in the open?

Well, except for that shrinkage bit.

"No. Have you got plans today? I was thinking of spending the day in bed. Naked."

"Sounds absolutely perfect, honey. I could spend a few thousand hours exploring you."

"You say the best things." Sid hooked a hand around his neck. "Show me that kissing thing again?"

"Yes, sir." He was chuckling as he leaned in, and their kiss tasted bitter and sweet -- the best coffee. Lord help him he didn't have to worry about anything, just loving on Sid and kissing the ever-loving fuck out of him.

"Mmm." The kiss he got in return was interested, warm, but not rushed. Sid took time, exploring his lips, his tongue. Made his heart beat heavily. "Taste so good."

"I was just thinking you taste like the perfect cup of coffee. Can we do it again?"

"I've got all day." Sid tugged the comforter free, then shifted and straddled his lap making the swing rock. "It's warming up out here. Or maybe that's the heater. Or you."

"Six of one, half dozen of the other." He got himself a double handful, humming in the back of his throat.

Sid kissed him again, but it took a while to get there, starting first with gentle nips at his jaw, then a teasing lick along his bottom lip. He groaned and followed those touches, kissing skin whenever he had a chance.

"This is crazy, right?" Sid caught his eyes, the green in the hazel shining happily in the sunlight. "It's not just me? I mean good-crazy, but crazy."

"Good crazy is my stock in trade, honey." Life was too fucking short to not be chasing the crazy with both feet, and he knew it.

"It's not mine. Not usually. But it is now." Sid took his face in both hands and kissed him hard, like patience wasn't a virtue they needed anymore. He grunted into the kiss, his stitches pulling a bit, but not hurting enough to want this to stop. Not for a second.

He dragged Sid into him, both of them hard as rocks, both of them needing again.

"Fuck, baby." Sid rocked into him. "Take me to bed?"

"God yes. Come hide under the covers with me, and let's

tear it up." Mackey stood up, lifting Sid up off his feet. He couldn't carry Sid, but he could lift him.

"Damn, cowboy." Sid blinked at him. "That was hot as hell."

"Good." He squeezed Sid's ass and let him down easy. "Come to bed. I want you." He wanted to stroke and pet and lick and fuck.

Sid nodded and led the way, undressing as they got inside, tossing his shirt first and then his sweats. The bed was still unmade, and it sounded like it was going to stay that way all day.

Good thing Mackey was all about that. They could change the sheets tonight and toss them in the washer.

"Damn, you got a pretty ass." He sat on the edge of the bed, cupping that sweet butt in both hands.

"Thank you. You've seen enough to know, I'm sure."

"I have. Good thing I know enough to admire." He licked the small of Sid's back, letting his tongue drag over the skin.

"Mmm." Sid leaned into the touch, looking over one shoulder at him. "I like how you admire."

"Just remember, I'm choosing to be right here with you now." This time he let his teeth scrape over Sid's skin, teasing a little bit.

"I know, Mackey. I'm looking forward to being reminded, though." Sid turned, kissed him quickly and climbed up on the bed.

He turned to slide into the covers, pulling the comforter over the top of them. Then he grabbed Sid and dragged him in close. He wasn't sure he could pinpoint the moment when Sid had turned from stranger to fantasy, but that was fine with him. He believed that God delivered what and who you needed, and he needed.

"Yeah." Sid arched and hooked a leg over his ass,

grinding against him. Oh, hello. His hands found what was absolutely their new favorite spot, that taut little ass.

"Want you to fuck me, baby." Sid's teeth found his shoulder, and bit down solid but not so hard to mark.

It felt like electricity hit Mackey -- body and brain. He could get aboard that particular train and ride until neither one of them could move.

Sid let him go and twisted under him, reaching for the nightstand. "Where's your... in here? Bathroom?"

"Yeah, it's in there. Let me..." Because of course, his favorite dildo and stroke mag was in that same drawer.

"I think I got it." Sid pulled the drawer open.

Oh, what the fuck? The man knew he wasn't dead or celibate. "The blue bottle. Got rubbers right there too."

Sid didn't even make a remark, just tossed him the bottle and moved his dildo out of the way to find the rubbers. "Found 'em." Sid ripped the wrapper open and tossed it, then reached for his happy prick to roll it on.

"You going to ride me, honey? Show me what all you've learned from the old west?" He panted a bit, telling himself this wasn't the hottest fucking thing on earth and that he could hold out.

"Yeehaw." Sid rolled again, pushed Mackie onto his back and grinned down at him. "I'm a natural. I already lassoed a cowboy, right? I think I can do better than eight seconds."

"I sure as shit hope so, honey. I want to watch you ride for days." He slicked his fingers up, letting them shine with lube. "Come here and let me get you ready."

"Hmm." Sid straddled him, facing away, presenting that pale and perfect ass. "How's that, cowboy?"

"Mmm..." He couldn't argue with that, and he sure as hell didn't intend to. He cupped Sid's backside with one hand and circled the tiny hole with his slick finger, teasing a second before he pressed inside.

Sid hissed and spread wider. "Ooh. Cold. Mmm." Hot fingers wrapped around his prick, stroking firmly.

"You say if you need me to slow down, honey. I wouldn't hurt you for the world." He liked to play hard, but not with a brand-new lover.

"What happened to 'let's tear it up'? I liked the sound of that." Sid arched harder for him.

Mackey tilted his head and pressed a second finger in, curling them and dragging them inside Sid until he heard the gasp he was hunting. Then he grinned and focused in on that spot. "I can handle that."

"Fuck. Yeah, you can." Oh, listen to the strain in that voice. Sid's fingers swept down under Mackey's balls and stroked a line back toward his hole.

He focused on driving Sid out of his mind, stroking steady and sure, his smile growing as Sid began to pant.

Sid groaned and lurched forward away from his fingers, then flipped around, green eyes focusing on him. "Fuck. Want you."

"Right here, pretty." He grabbed Sid's hips, his lips pulling away from his teeth when Sid grabbed his cock. Oh damn, that was fine.

Sid rocked against him, rubbing his prick across a willing hole, and then slowly sank down, never looking away for a second. Mackey pushed inside that sweet heat, both of them groaning as Sid relaxed, stretching to let him past the tight muscle. He sucked in a breath, waiting to brace himself on the bed until Sid was settled against him, ass tight around him.

"Mackey." Sid paused, took a breath, let it out slow, then

took him in deep until Sid was seated flush against his hips. "God. So full."

"Mmm." He didn't have any words, but he didn't need any. He needed to focus on holding himself together. His hands opened and closed, and as soon as Sid relaxed again, he rocked them hard.

"Fuck!" Sid's hands landed on his chest, fingers digging into his skin, and went a little wild, slamming down to meet him, riding him like they didn't have all day. Sid's brow furrowed with the effort, but those eyes never left his. They held on, steady, letting Mackey see right into that need.

Mackey found the rhythm, focusing on thrusting up, pulling down, over and over, giving Sid the ride he wanted. Sid was tight enough to make him whimper, and if he had been a weaker man, he would have shot. He was a cowboy, though, so he held on by the skin of his teeth.

Sid shivered and tossed his head back, finally breaking that stare. "Touch me, baby. Please? So close." The words were delivered on quick, panting breaths. "Just... touch me."

He didn't answer. He grabbed Sid's cock and started jacking good and hard. *Come on, baby. Show me.*

"Yeah. Yes!" It didn't take a second. Sid went tight around his cock first, making them both groan, and Sid's face went hot red as he shot, spraying over his fist and onto his chest.

Mackey managed to breathe, to watch Sid's face for a few breaths before his own need took over. He groaned, slamming up into Sid, driving himself higher and faster, letting his muscles work like they were supposed to.

Best he could tell Sid loved it. His lover bore down on him, reaching back and holding onto his thigh with one hand and working his own prick with the other, eyes on him again.

"Jesus." The son of a bitch was beautiful. Absolutely

fucking stunning. His eyes rolled back in his head, and he let himself go, let himself fuck Sid's ass until all he could do was roar and shoot.

"Fuck." Sid fell forward, panting hard, forehead coming to rest on his shoulder. "Holy fuck."

"Yeah." He could get behind that, sure enough.

Sid chuckled and moved, stretching out long beside him and dropping kisses on his shoulder. "You're the hottest thing I've ever seen."

He kissed Sid's temple before managing to get the rubber off and tossed, and then he settled back with a soft sigh, letting Sid snuggle in. "Damn."

"Mmhm." Soft lips closed over his. Sid's kiss was gentle but not lazy, curious, almost like it was asking him for something. He smiled and opened up to it, one hand on Sid's hip. He sighed and relaxed, letting Sid in.

Sid tasted, explored, and stretched the kiss for a long while, finally humming at him and sounding satisfied. Sid rested on his chest, on arm over his waist. "Mmm. Good."

"Oh, better than that, I think."

That got him a chuckle. "Better. I'm starting to really like you, Maverick."

No one called him Maverick. No one. It made him hug Sid tight and kiss the man's temple again. "You think? Wait until I put you to work up here."

"I think. Also, you can't threaten me. I already offered." Sid was drawing patterns on his skin, circling scars and tracing his ribs with a warm finger. "Although it's tempting to just sit and stare at you. I could watch you move all day."

"Listen to you." His cheeks were on fire. He'd never had a guy that…talked pretty to him.

"What? You're handsome, Maverick. Graceful." Sid

looked up into his eyes seriously. "And your eyes are out of this world."

"You're...damn, babe." He took a hard kiss, because he didn't know what to say. Who did? It felt so...romantic.

Sid met him halfway, returning the kiss. He could feel Sid's heart pounding against him, everything about Sid so real and present. Focused.

It was more than a little addicting, if he was gonna be honest.

When they finally parted, Sid was flushed and breathless and stared into him for a long, quiet moment. The look was hard to read, but it ended with a quirky smile and a nod. Sid lay down on his chest and tucked an arm around him but didn't seem to know what to say right now either.

Whatever they needed to say, it could wait. They were here now and resting together. It was enough. He reached for that fine ass, laid a hand there and closed his eyes.

19

Sid woke up completely buried by cowboy. There was a cowboy leg over his thighs making sure he stayed put, a cowboy arm curled around him like he needed protection, and an actual cowboy pressed tightly against his back.

He'd never been happier to be anywhere in his entire life.

Mackey--Maverick--he'd decided he was going to use his lover's real name if they were going to be more than coworkers--*Maverick* smelled so... it was hard to put a word to it. Manly? Masculine. Like the outdoors, and hard work, and a buttload of testosterone. Maybe the word was just cowboy. Whatever he called it, it was new to Sid, and he liked it.

He liked Maverick too. A lot more than he thought he probably should, but he wasn't going to worry about that. Maverick was like a fantasy come true and, at the same time, one of the realest people he'd ever met. He was fascinated. Totally charmed. Seduced. He was good with all of it.

Sid was sore in all the right ways. He'd be feeling Maverick all day for sure. That was a fuck for the record books. One he wouldn't forget even after he wasn't walking funny.

Sid tried to stretch, but it wasn't easy. Not that he was complaining. He was ready to stay right here until something drove them out of bed. Probably Maverick's stomach. It wouldn't be long; the sun was lower so it had to be well into the day already.

Maverick sighed against his neck, the sound low and easy. The hug was tight for a second, almost stealing his breath, then it eased up.

"Mhm." He liked that. He hummed softly and tangled their fingers. "You got me. I'm right here, baby."

"Better than it just bein' a dream." Maverick nuzzled against his shoulder blades, and it blew his mind, the juxtaposition of hard cowboy and gentle man.

"Much better, and I love how you sleep. You must have good dreams too." Still and quiet, trusting, and all over him.

"I do. My happy ass is here with you. I've had some of the best sex of my life, and we're still figuring each other out. I'm not hurting too bad. Life is fucking good, honey."

"Best sex of your life, huh?" Sid turned back to grin at Maverick. "I bet you say that to all the buckle bunnies."

Maverick's grin was slow and wicked. "No, sir. I give credit where credit is due. And I'm too old and thick to attract either the bunnies or the buddies."

"Oh, the poor fools. You're thick all right. Just not where they can see." He rocked back with his hips, loving that perfect ache. "Mmm."

Maverick's lips brushed his ear. "You know how hot you are, moving like that? You make me want to turn you inside out."

"Fuck, Mav." Fire flew up his spine, and he shivered, Maverick's words lighting up every nerve. Did the cowboy know him that well already? There was really only one possible response to words like that, so he did it again.

Maverick groaned, teeth grazing his earlobe hard enough to sting. One hand slid up his body to tease his nipple, the other teased his ass.

Sid hissed, and there was no stopping the little whimper that escaped him as he tried to concentrate on all of that sensation at once.

"Oh, pretty, you make me ache." Maverick began to tap his hole, just hard enough that it jolted through his entire body.

That makes two of us.

That tone made him feel a little wicked, and his moan came out more of a growl. He bent his knee, opening to that touch. Fuck, the cowboy had good hands. Mav could turn him inside out, upside down, any way he wanted as long as it felt this good. "Yeah? You want me, baby?"

"I do." That finger disappeared, then before he could complain, returned slick and cold, easing inside him.

He huffed out a breath because he was still so sensitive. He did love that burn though. "Jesus." He bent that knee up farther and tangled his fingers in the sheets.

"Just breathe, pretty." Maverick finger fucked him, the rhythm firm and steady, almost hypnotizing.

He nodded. He could do that.

Maybe.

It was harder than he thought. Sid forced himself to take in a deep breath and it came back out in a long, low moan. "Mav."

"Yeah, pretty. I got you." One finger became two, but the steady motion didn't falter. It was like being caught in the ocean, the waves coming on and on.

"Mmm. Got me." Sid arched back to meet the touch,

caught up in his senses and the need that was building in him. "Baby. Please."

"I won't leave you hanging." It was hard to believe those thick, rough fingers could dance on his nerves like magic, but they were, and when Mav touched him just right, his entire body lit up.

He gasped and rocked into those fingers as his balls drew up, and everything tingled. "Fuck." Maverick had him so worked up he couldn't hold a thought in his head.

"Love watching this." Maverick never let up, never eased back. No, Mav demanded his complete pleasure.

"Just don't stop." He caught his aching cock in his fist and worked it just right, fingers gliding over his shaft and thumb just brushing the head. "Don't stop."

Maverick's voice was a deep growl, right by his ear. "Not gonna stop, pretty. Gonna make you come and come."

Oh God.

Oh, that totally worked for him. Sid rolled his hips willing Mav to hit that spot again… and he did.

Fireworks went off behind his eyelids, all the air seemed to leave the room, and it felt like he shot for days, his whole body contracting with it.

Mav kept tapping, stroking, and his balls kept emptying until he wanted to scream.

"*Mav.*" He gulped in air, but he was frozen, caught between wanting to get away from that relentless touch and wanting more. He whimpered, begging for something--he didn't even know what. He knew it sounded pitiful, but he just didn't care.

"Breathe, pretty. I have you. I won't let you fall." The words echoed inside him, with this amazing, deep calm that matched the steady touches inside him.

He trusted that because... because he wanted to, and tried to breathe, but it was shaky at best. "God. Can't, baby."

"Sweet..." The touches eased, letting him relax, leaving him wrung out and boneless.

Sid moaned as those fingers left him, and he sank into the mattress feeling so heavy, like he weighed a thousand pounds. He tried another deep breath and managed it this time, a whole world of satisfaction in his exhale.

"Mmm..." Maverick nuzzled his shoulder and held him close. "So good."

He breathed Maverick in, feeling like the cowboy had touched his soul instead of his trigger. That voice, so deliberate, seductive, so fucking undeniable. Nobody had ever done that to him, and it was hottest fucking thing ever. "You...fuck, Mav."

He snorted, which was about all the energy he had to laugh at himself. Bad enough he couldn't move, but he couldn't speak either.

"Mmm...Just rest with me, pretty. You had one hell of a morning."

He wasn't going to take much convincing, because that sounded like the best idea ever. Just rest, right here in Maverick's arms.

He thought he could do that. He closed his eyes and that was the last thing he thought as the world went dark.

20

Mackey whistled as he made burgers on the indoor grill, knowing that eventually the scent would wake up his own personal Sleeping Beauty. He had loved the fuck out of this morning, watching Sid come undone.

Now he felt studly and strong and sensual as fuck.

"Make mine rare, baby!" His lover's voice came from above, where Sid was leaning over the loft railing, bare-chested in blue jeans, hair combed and damp. "Do you have bacon? I'm starving."

"I made it in the microwave. You want cheese?" He grinned up, feeling like a super-D cowboy.

"Yes, please. I'll be right down. The stairs are going to be a challenge." Sid laughed, the sound happy, and little scratchy, probably from, well, all the shouting of his name.

"Just take it easy. Don't break that pretty heinie." He had plans for Sid, front and back. Forward and aft?

"Don't you worry. I'm not a bullfighter, but I'm tougher than I look." Sid pushed off the railing and disappeared.

He chuckled and pulled off Sid's burgers, popping

cheese on top and putting the lids on. He had all the fixings out, plus chips and dip. Lunch of champions.

When Sid reappeared he'd pulled on a well-worn Nine Inch Nails long sleeved T-shirt over those low-riding jeans. He was moving better than he'd made it sound, but there was definitely a little hitch in his stride.

Sid hesitated in the doorway and let him look. "I could eat."

"Good. Take your plate, so I can pull off my burgers." He handed the dish over and took a long, hard kiss. "Afternoon, pretty."

Sid smiled, looking bewildered by his kiss. "Afternoon, bright eyes. It warmed up a little, huh? It looks gorgeous out there. Perfect in here."

"It is perfect. The sun is melting the snow a little bit. I think we should run into town before the next snow, get ourselves a Christmas tree to bring home." The longer he spent here, the happier he got.

Sid's gaze dragged over him, looking him right up and down, lingering here and there, then flicked up to meet his. "This view is spectacular."

Oh good lord. He blushed, heat climbing up his chest and heating his cheeks.

Sid winked and turned a shoulder to him, flirting. "Bacon in the microwave you said?"

"I did. And there's mayonnaise, mustard, and ketchup in the fridge."

"Thanks, handsome." He got a maddeningly chaste peck on the cheek and then Sid headed for the fridge with his plate.

"I'll be right there." He just needed to rescue his burgers before they turned to charcoal. He grabbed the patties, turned off the grill, and scrubbed it down with a cloth.

Sid had set out all the fixings on the kitchen island by the time he got done, and the kitchen table had two places set, like with napkins and everything.

Sid leaned on the counter while he set up his burgers. "I started to raid your beer but thought I should ask first. You want one?"

"Hell, yeah. Burgers, chips, beer — life is good. I'm thinking on making a big pot of chili tonight." He winked at Sid. "And you're welcome to raid what you will, honey. Make yourself at home."

"Awesome." Sid wandered over to the fridge and pulled out two beers. "She really stocks this place for you. So cool."

"Well, the closest stores are in Telluride, so you have to plan, right?" In fact, he needed to start a list.

"That's a drive, huh? Then I guess so." Sid opened the beers and set them down on the table. "I'm about to inhale these. My morning took it out of me."

"You were busy-busy." And he'd enjoyed every second of it. He liked to watch Sid's face when he was lost to hunger.

"You had me out of my mind. I was just... whoa. Gone." Sid's smile was shy but not embarrassed. Mackey could hear the honesty. "I owe you an orgasm."

"I'm not keeping count, but if you're offering, I'm not going to be all 'no, no, I don't want to be loved on'."

"Always good to have something to look forward to." Sid took an enormous bite of his burger and did a little chair dance. "Mm-M."

Oh, excellent. He tucked in, chowing down on the burgers.

It was something else, watching Sid swallow down an entire burger before he stopped chewing long enough to speak again. Mackey took it as a compliment.

Sid licked his fingers looking a little sheepish. "Told you I was hungry. That was so good."

"I made you two. Breakfast was scant." He moved around enough that he ate what and when he wanted to.

"Breakfast... that feels like yesterday." Sid laughed and doctored up his second burger. "I'm going to have to run or something. Are we going to get to work on that room after lunch?"

"Sounds like a plan. There's a construction dumpster around back to, well, dump." It was a little exciting, honestly, because there was everything from furniture to clothes to weird toys to newspapers up there. He wanted to know what was hiding, what the bones looked like. Everything.

"And that whole floor is going to be a suite? Or do you have different plans for that room?" Sid ate this burger more slowly, taking a bite and savoring it a bit. "Mmm."

"The whole floor is going to be a huge suite. Somewhere I can hide when all the guys come over and won't leave." He could keep his space locked and private and not seem mean.

"That's going to be amazing. Are you planning on hiring someone in to do some of it? Or are you going do it all yourself?" Sid snagged a chip and popped it in his mouth.

"I've got a contractor to work while I'm on the road next year." He didn't want to waste a ton of time. "He'll do the major parts for me."

"Nice. So we'll get the upstairs all cleaned up for him then before we head out for the city." Sid stopped, blushed dark. "I mean, if you want me here that long."

"Don't act any dumber than you have to, honey. You're welcome here." In fact, Sid was more than just welcome. Mackey squeezed Sid's fingers. Shit, he was sleeping with a suit, and he was loving it. His boys were going to ride his ass like a prized pony. "Although I hope you put shit together with your daddy, for your sake. Maybe he'll come up to the big show while we're up there?"

"Maybe." Sid stroked his hand. "Who knows if he'll come. He and I are kind of back and forth, you know? He's a tough guy to please."

"Yeah? You're doing damn good for yourself, though. He has to like that." He would be damn proud if Sid was his son. Sad, because he felt totally non-paternal feelings about the man, but proud, nonetheless.

"He doesn't really know what I do. He didn't like that I moved to New York, mostly because I came out to him before I left and refused to let him set me up with any more of his friends' daughters." Sid laughed but it didn't light up those eyes the way it should.

"Ah." Oh, he knew all about that shit. "I never came out like that. I mean, I'm not like some guys — I know I'm gay. I know I like dick, but I never told my kin, for just that reason."

"I didn't really mean to. We had an argument, and I kind of blurted it out." Sid snorted and frowned at his beer bottle. "I don't know if I won the argument, but it shut him up. I stayed home for a year after that, and it was really quiet in the house."

He knew about that too, but he'd told Sid that story. "Well, your life ain't real quiet now, is it?"

Sid smiled, and green eyes flicked up and met his. "No. I have an incredible job. And I've met the most amazing guy. He's a cowboy. You'd like him. He's hotter than a New York City sidewalk in July. There's no being quiet around him."

"So long as he's tough as a bullfighter, you'll be okay with him, I reckon." He wasn't sure anyone'd ever called him hot before, but it sure felt good to hear.

Sid's voice dropped low, eyes narrowing. "Oh, I am not safe around him at all."

"No?" Oh, he felt that, deep in the pit of his belly. Sid made him feel shit that no one else had. Ever. "You don't think?"

"Not at all. I don't even want to be." Sid's eyes were on him, even as his lover sipped his beer.

"Damn, honey. You make me ache inside." His cheeks were burning, but he was tickled shitless.

"Good. Keep that feeling for the day, and I'll make it worth your while tonight." Sid winked, drained the rest of the beer, and changed the subject like Mackey wasn't nursing half a hard-on. "Your burgers were amazing. Thank you. I was really hungry."

"You're welcome. They came out okay, I thought. I got the chili for tonight. It'll do us for a day or two. Then we'll smoke a turkey for Christmas, if you want. Or do a roast. I'm easy."

"Oh, yum. You're going to make me fat." Sid laughed and cleared their plates. "I'll take today off, but tomorrow I better run."

"In the snow? Good luck. I run the stairs a lot." It damn near killed his ankle, but he kept that to himself.

"Worried a bear is going to eat you?" Sid moved around his kitchen like he belonged here, putting condiments away and doing dishes.

"No. No, more worried if I get out there and get lost, I'll freeze to death overnight." He had a lot to learn about living up here, and he knew it. "Also, your legs are taller than mine."

"Well, we'll see how it goes. I'll stay on the road once I find it, and I'll bring my phone. No worries. I'm not going to explore, at least not without you. If it's too slippery I won't get far anyway."

"I'm going to put in a workout room too, I think. For when the snows are high." Because they'd get worse. A treadmill, bike, free weights — everything a man could need.

"Yeah? Awesome. You certainly have the room." Sid moved in behind him and put steady hands on his shoulders, thumbs working gently into the muscle there. "Ready to get to work?"

"Uh-huh." Right. With that touch making his arms feel heavy and stupid. Totally. Working. "Let me put shit back in the fridge. Pick some music?"

"Kitchen's done, baby. I even loaded the dishwasher." Sid fingers were finding little hot spots and working them. "Were you watching me or my ass all that time?"

"I—" Well, fuck him raw. "I got no idea what you're talking about." He grinned though, and blushed hot as blazes. "I might have been woolgathering and admiring."

"You make me feel pretty sexy, cowboy. I've never known anyone who liked looking at me so much." Sid didn't sound self-conscious at all. "I like it."

"Yeah? Excellent." Because he could watch Sid for hours. The man fascinated the living fuck out of him.

Sid kissed the side of his neck, behind his ear, his temple. The touches were feather-light, the farthest thing from what he got in the arena, from men and bulls.

"You do make me feel good, honey. Swear to God." He reached back and grabbed Sid's hip, enjoying the slow throb of arousal. "Want to explore upstairs?"

"Yeah, let's do it." That got him a thump on the shoulder, and Sid moved around him, heading for the stairs. "What are you going to do in this foyer? It's huge. Maybe some couches?"

"Yeah, something cushy and leather, but washable. You know the guys. They can be tough on stuff." But he liked the idea of those...what did they call them? Not sectionals... "You seen them couch-deals that can be all sorts of shapes?"

"Like, modular? You can move the pieces around? That's a great idea." Sid looked over his shoulder, tucked one hand into a back pocket and headed up the stairs ahead of him. Letting him watch.

Butthead. Fuck, that was something else. "Gonna make you scream for me tonight, pretty."

Sid made him a little growly, in the hungry sort of way.

"Mmm. I hope so." Sid stopped at the top of the stairs and waited for him. "But I'm going to drive you out of your mind first. I'm going to make you work for it."

"I ain't scairt of hard work, pretty. Not a bit." In fact, he was pretty damn good at it.

"Good, because I think we have some waiting for us in that room."

"Yeah, it's..." Blah. Yeah. "It'll be easier with an extra pair of hands."

He rubbed the stitches on his chin, telling them to stop itching. The skin in there was still real red, so he couldn't take them out yet. Maybe in a couple days.

"Does that hurt? You haven't told me how you're feeling, but you don't seem to need your pain meds..." Sid stepped into the room and looked around with a whistle. "Okay, this is a mess, but look at those windows."

He didn't bother to answer. He hurt. That was part of his job. "Right? There's a balcony on this side too. I was tickled that the glass was all intact."

Sid ran a comforting hand down his back as if his lover

knew what he wasn't saying. "If you took that wall down there and opened it up to the rest of the upstairs, and then just re-stained all this wood, this would be a really nice living room kind of thing. You could get rid of that tiny bathroom and put in a wet bar and a little fridge."

"Oh, that would be cool. I like the idea of a coffee bar up here, maybe even a toaster oven."

"Mmm. Breakfast in bed. English muffin pizzas on the deck. Hot coffee at arm's length? Works for me." Sid waded right in, making a path down the middle of the room. There were boxes of papers and books, some old furniture and lamps. Just a mass of things to go through.

"Keep the books. I like to read, and I bet we'll need reading material this winter."

Sid reached for a stack of books and brushed their hips together as he passed. "We, huh?"

"I--" Fuck. That was a slip and a half. "Sue me. I like the idea of you, naked and in the bed, fire going, snow everywhere. I like the idea of you on the balcony sunbathing in the spring."

Sid set the books down against the wall and smiled for him. "It sounds good to me too, I just wanted to know if you'd said it on purpose."

"Yeah. I did." Why lie? He was allowed to have a hint of dork to him, wasn't he?

Sid drew a hand slowly over his ribs on the way back to the boxes. "I thought cowboys were supposed to be in love with their trucks and their horses and would leave their lovers crying in their beer. That's how the songs go, right?"

"Lots of 'em, yeah. Lots are about happier things. Loved a lot of horses over the years, though. Been riding since before I could walk." He winked at Sid and pulled out enough folding chairs to seat a wedding.

"I guess we'll just have to see how it goes then." Sid chuckled warmly. "Those will come in handy for your next barbecue; they'll seat a lot of cowboy butts."

"Yeah. I'll take them out to the shed." Thank God for covered walkways. He started taking them, four at a time. Down the stairs, out to the shed, up the stairs, get more chairs.

By the time he was done, he was sweating like a whore in church, and his leg was grumping at him, but he headed up to see what was next.

Sid had the room sorted, cardboard boxes all against one wall, a stack of books piled against another. Sid was stretched out on a bright green fainting couch, flipping pages in what looked like a photo album. His lover glanced up as he stepped into the room.

"Everything in those boxes on the left is pretty much garbage. The two smaller boxes have weird stuff--a couple of beer steins, a tea pot, a couple of board games. I unburied this great couch covered in hideous fabric and pictures!"

"That's amazing." He didn't even mind the green. "If it's in good shape, I'll keep it."

Okay. Boxes. He grabbed two of the trash boxes and hefted them. "I'll be back."

"Oh. Hang on, I'll help." Sid put the book down and hopped to his feet. "Right behind you."

"If you'll just leave yours at the bottom of the stairs, I'll run them out once they're all down from up there." Sid had made things look amazing in short order.

"I can do that." Sid set his boxes down and headed back upstairs. There were a lot of them, some of them heavier than others. It was hard to believe that anyone would leave an entire room full of junk behind. But the couch was a good find.

He put his head down and got to work, just pushing through. He was earning his steak, sure as shit.

Sid helped him get the last two loads out to the dumpster, and he knew he was being watched. Sid had been around him long enough there was no real hiding when he needed a break. "How about we get a beer and breathe a minute? It's getting dark and cold as fuck."

"Sounds like a plan." He grabbed a bandana from his back pocket and wiped his face, because damn, he was dripping and he was a little afraid he'd form icicles on the end of his nose. "There's Shiners in the beer cooler out here."

Maybe he needed coffee.

"You're prepared, huh?" Sid headed for the cooler and pulled two out, even found the opener on the string. "So... you look like you're hurting, baby." Sid held a cold bottle up to his cheek.

Oh fuck. That sudden cold made him feel like throwing up. He wouldn't. He wouldn't even flinch, but damn. "Little bit. Thank you for your help. That's a cool couch, huh?"

"It's in pretty good shape too. I think if I give the upholstery a good scrub it might actually be not so hideous." Sid sipped his beer. "Mmm. That's good. It has turned legs; they just need refinishing."

"Good deal. I've found a couple of nice pieces in here."

Sid got him inside in the heat and pushed a kitchen chair over. "Sit, baby. Tell me what I can do to make it better."

"Better? You did a ton." He sat, though, because damn he was tired.

"I meant for you. Get you your meds? Shoulder rub, maybe?" Sid stood close and rested a hand on his arm.

"Oh, just touch me a second, pretty. You got hands that make me happy as a dog with two tails."

"That's happy all right." Sid set his beer down, pulled up another chair to sit on and icy hands went up under his shirt, fingers sliding over his skin, making his muscles bunch and shudder. "So when you're hurting... I mean, I know about the headaches, but what hurts exactly?"

"Mostly? My damn leg. The thigh is metal, but I got a bad ankle, and there's no fixin' that." It was part of the game, all the way.

"What do you usually do for it?" Those hands spread across his skin, fingers finally warming and fanning out over his shoulder blades. "Heat? Cold? Tequila?"

"I got a whole taping, ice-heating pad, salve, tens-unit routine. Shit, I have a whole suitcase of 'don't die on the dirt' prevention."

"Wow. Okay." Sid started rubbing, digging into tight spots here and there.

"Right? We're a beat-up motley group."

"And I thought getting dressed down by Brad over that blackout was painful." Sid chuckled. "He's such an ass."

"Lord, he's something, and he hates me like no one else. It's fucking amazing." There was nothing he could do about it. He'd been in the right. He wasn't going to kiss the bastard's ass because that was political.

"I told him I was flattered that he thought I was talented enough to turn the lights back on with sheer will power. He snorted and hung up on me. I don't think we're friends." Sid's thumb hit a knot and dug in hard.

He grunted softly, his toes curling as his nerves fired, shooting down his arm. "He ain't no one's friend, pretty."

"Literally no one has ever called me 'pretty.'"

"No? I can't believe that." Sid was fine as frog hair and twice as shiny.

Sid laughed. "Believe it, cowboy."

"Well, I cain't help that you been around lots of dipshits. I could watch you for hours."

"That can be arranged." Sid leaned on his shoulder, arms circling around his waist. "You make me feel 'pretty.' Sexy."

"Good." That was sort of his job, right? A man deserved to feel like he was the hottest thing on earth, so far as he was concerned.

"Are you ready to go through more stuff upstairs? Or do you want to take a break and maybe tell me about what's around the property?"

"Oh, there's a damn fine amount to see. There's barns, out buildings, and trails. I want to see if there's good fishing."

"Cool." Sid leaned back with his beer, smiling at him." I haven't been fishing in forever. I'm not sure I remember how to sit still that long."

"They tell me that I need to learn to fly fish. There's a stream running through the property with rainbow trout." He stood up, suddenly so thirsty it hurt. He grabbed two bottles of water out of the fridge and handed one over to Sid.

"That sounds like fun. Is it a thing you teach yourself? It seems like something you'd want an instructor for." Sid finished off his beer and opened the water, taking his hint. "Grilled trout sounds like a plan."

"I intend to find out this spring. The realtor I worked with, her husband ties flies, so I think maybe I'll ask him if he could help a cowboy out." Surely that would work.

"Maybe he has some time this week? I'd love to learn,

and tying flies is something I could do on the road that isn't playing on my phone." Sid headed around to the back door, looking out towards where the elk they'd seen this morning had been grazing.

"I'll holler over to Helen and ask." He didn't see why not. He'd bet both Helen and her man had some great stories to tell.

"Cool. Is the barn in good shape?"

He wandered over and patted Sid's butt. "The horse barns are in good shape. The hay barns need a little help."

"Are you going to keep horses after you retire?"

"You know it. I want horses, llamas, maybe some donkeys." He loved critters, and he was good with them.

"Llamas? People keep llamas? I've only ever seen them in a zoo." Sid seemed a little bit like a kid in a candy store.

"Really? Huh." Weird. "It's gorgeous up here, isn't it? I love the wood and the smell and...everything."

"Wow. Do you have to...store the other guy's horses?"

So goddamn cute. "Board, and yeah, for Jack. He comes up here a lot, when he's passing through, and he leaves his horses."

"Jack." Sid nodded. "Seems like a good guy."

"Jack is probably the best buddy I got." Mackey met Sid's eyes, because he'd want to know how the cow ate the cabbage if he was Sid. "We tried to be a thing for about seven seconds, and I admit to calling him for relief, but he's not interested in ever being one guy's. Not ever. One day, I want to retire and be part of an us, dumb as that sounds."

Sid's head tilted slightly, and he got a curious smile. "Why does that sound dumb? Isn't that kind of the point?"

"Well yeah, I guess it is." He'd always just worried that no one would want what all he had to offer on the long term.

"I'm looking forward to rocking chairs, a good view and an old dog. Someone to complain about the Red Sox to. Shouting at kids to get off my lawn." Sid took his hand. "Someone to... what did you say? Read with in the wintertime."

"Yeah. Someone that you know, all the way." He craved that. He loved the idea of years and together and all. He knew a few guys that had it. Guys like him. So it wasn't impossible, right?

"It's not dumb. And you don't know if you can have it unless you try." Sid kissed his cheek. "Hurts like hell when it doesn't work out though. I've been there a couple of times."

"I can imagine." Mackey remembered when Jack had said that there wasn't anyone he wanted bad enough to stick with. Mackey had spent a bit in the bottle, and a bit taking his pleasure anywhere he could.

"I'd wondered about Jack. Truth? I saw him leaving your hotel room one morning and I assumed... He was literally still tucking in his shirt."

Mackey nodded. "Yeah. When I'm hurt bad, he'll stay a lot. Make sure I can make it in and out of the shower, help me with my TENS unit." Sometimes they were both just lonely and held on to someone that needed holding.

"Will you let me do that now?" Sid looked into his eyes and a hand slid into his back pocket.

Oh. Oh, sweet Jesus, yes. He wasn't sure how he'd gone from fighting to fucking to being fond, but he wasn't going to bitch. Sid had cared enough to bring him granddaddy's ring. "If you're willing, the job's yours."

"I'm willing. I've already seen you pretty fucked up, right? You're still pretty fucked up right now. I think I've got this."

"You haven't seen me at my worst, but close, yeah." The

worst had been the second broken neck. He'd begged to die, but the good Lord obviously wasn't ready.

Sid searched his eyes, and he had to wonder what his lover was seeing. "It's not really a competition, Maverick. We'll manage."

"What's not?" He was utterly confused. He wouldn't wish hurting on anyone, especially not Sid.

"I meant if that's the case, I don't need to see you at your worst, that's all."

"Ah. No, let's just not have that happen again. I'm tired of being beat up, some." Not that he was bitching, he wasn't. Much.

"Good." The fingers in his pocket curled against his ass. "What do you want to show me next?"

"We could go upstairs and look for the water. I want to see it." He wanted to explore, go see what they could see.

"Sounds like fun." Sid kept an arm around his back, and that hand stayed tucked firmly in his pocket.

"Probably a good idea. Thanks." Sid leaned against him, smiling. "So we can still fish in the winter? Cool. Too bad it doesn't freeze over, we could skate."

"We'll go to Telluride. They have everything." We. God, he loved that word. So bad.

"Yeah? I've never been anywhere out here except where I've been with the show. I'm happy to have you show me around."

"It's gorgeous. We'll drive out either tomorrow or the next day, have supper out, see the town." He hadn't explored much himself, and he was looking forward to it.

"Cool. Let's do some more work and then I'll help with the chili?" Sid gulped from the water bottle, then looped an arm around him as they wandered out of the kitchen.

"Sounds good to me. We should go through those boxes

still in the upstairs room. Or... did you see the humongous mirror in there? You should keep it. It should go in the bedroom."

"Yeah? Is it cool? We should keep the good stuff. You can tell I brought all I had, and the house needs the furniture." There it was again, that 'we'. He settled one hand at the small of Sid's back, trying that out.

Sid glanced at him. "Was it hard? Leaving your parents' house for good?"

Lord, how to answer that? "Yes and no? I wish that it had been harder. I wish that all the love hadn't been sucked from the land. This place is-- it's going to be heaven."

Sid leaned in and kissed his jaw. "It's almost heaven already."

"It is. It's a haven." A cowboy haven. Damn, he liked that.

"You should name it Haven *something...* or something-Haven. It's a big enough property to deserve a name. Think about it."

"Yeah. Yeah, I could have it put on the gate." He loved that. He really did. "I'm glad you're here."

And didn't that feel fine to say.

Sid stopped them at the base of the stairs and looked into his eyes. "I am too. I'm still a little dizzy about it, but I'm happy."

"That works. Happy works." He took a long, slow, easy kiss. "We work."

"We do. We shouldn't, but we do." Sid rocked on his heels and grabbed onto him for balance. "See dizzy. Jesus, that's a wild feeling."

"Let's get you more water, and we'll sit for a bit. Watch the mountains." They needed to chill and rest. Altitude was a bitch.

"You think it's the altitude? I'm giving you all the credit.

That was a nice kiss." Sid took his hand and trailed after him.

"You make my cheeks hot, pretty." No one had ever said those sorts of things to him before.

"I do? Well, I like making you feel good. It's been a good day, bright eyes."

"It has. Let me grab us more to drink, and we'll have some TV time. The water finding can wait, it's not going anywhere." He was ready to sit, hang out, possibly nap.

Probably nap.

"You know, that sounds perfect. Movie? Music?"

"Let's put on a movie that no one minds if we sleep through."

Sid gave him a soft smile, eyes already half-lidded. "Mhm. Works for me. Which couch?"

"Mine in the family room. It has magic fingers and two recliners. Cup holders." He led the way.

"Oh man. That's not a couch, that's a Cadillac." Sid spun around and sat, stretching his arms out. "It's big, Mav."

"That's what everyone says, pretty." He turned on the vibrations on his recliner.

"Everyone huh?" Sid grinned over at him. "I bet that feels good."

His answer was to flex before they both cracked up. "Here's the remote, pretty. Have at."

He was damn near asleep already.

Sid turned it on and flipped to the Discovery Channel. "Whales," Sid said, yawning and kicking back in the other recliner.

"I like whales…" And he loved his napping couch.

21

Sid climbed out of Maverick's truck in Telluride and stared down the main drag, all wide-eyed and astonished by...everything. The historic-looking town with all its shops, the snow-covered mountain in the distance, and all the twinkling lights, red bows and greenery of the holidays. "Mav...this is amazing. Gorgeous."

It was so picture postcard perfect, so romantic that he wanted to throw his arms around Mav and kiss him. Make a little Christmas postcard of their own.

"Yeah..." Mav was as open-mouthed as he felt, looking around like a kid in a toy store. "It's like magic."

He took hold of one of Mav's pinky fingers with one of his own. "It's so beautiful. It makes me want to kiss you." He let go quickly because Maverick was kind of a celebrity, and he wasn't sure how that played out in a place like this.

"Does it?" Mav grinned at him, the look wolfish, and tugged him into the lee of a building, kissing him hard enough his ears rang.

"Well, that was something." Sid nodded, cheeks flaming and breathless from the kiss.

"It is. And I'm thankful for each second of it, swear to God." And look at that wondering, wondrous smile.

"Me too. You can do that any time." He tangled his fingers with Maverick's. "So, what's the deal here? Can I... can we?" He squeezed Maverick's fingers. "Or does the whole world know you here too?"

"No one knows me here, not really. I'm not at work. You can. We can. If the league bitches, I'll take them down." Mav sounded completely, totally serious. Just totally.

He couldn't hold back his grin, or the surge of pure joy that made him steal another quick, happy kiss. He wanted to be a couple with Maverick, and act like one. He was proud of his brave cowboy and this unexpected but wonderful thing they had going. But it was important—a rule—to never out anyone for any reason, even a happy reason like this, and if Mav had said he wasn't ready, or it wasn't comfortable, Sid would have willingly respected that. The bull riding profession wasn't generally a safe space, and Maverick had a right to his privacy.

This was better though. This was so much fucking better.

He squeezed Mav's fingers again and pulled his lover back onto the sidewalk, boldly holding hands like he would with a lover back in New York. "So where first?"

Mav glanced around, then grinned. "There's a Patagonia. Let's get you socks and some longies so your dick don't freeze."

"Oh, you're dressing me now?" That sounded like a good idea, though. He had a coat that was probably okay, but just jeans weren't going to cut it. Life was cold at this altitude.

"I'm protecting my investment." He got a wicked grin, and his ass received a firm goosing. "Come on. Let's get you suited up. You ever try snowboarding?"

"Nope. I don't think I'm cool enough to snowboard. You? I bet you want to try it." Maverick was a risk-taker. He probably wanted to try everything.

"Yeah. Let's get a snowboard. How hard can it be? I mean, not the tricks, just the zooming." How could anyone — anyone — resist the excitement in those eyes?

"How hard can it be? That seems like a dangerous question. I'm going to have bruises to match yours. What size long-johns do I need?" He grabbed a package, looking for his size. It was a diversion though; he knew they'd be walking out of here with a snowboard.

Maverick sized him up. "Large, or a medium extra tall. I wear a large in the pants and an XL across the chest."

He found the large and went looking for socks. "I think you need to buy boots with that snowboard."

"Oh, is that a thing?" Mav called over the salesperson, and in a matter of minutes had them set up with cold-weather gear, boots, and a snowboard.

"Good thing I have a subletter in my apartment, huh?" He pulled out his credit card. It was pricey, but he really liked the new coat they'd found.

"I'll get the snowboarding stuff and the longies, since they're protecting something for me." Oh, that was a wicked wink.

"I think I can handle my own underwear, cowboy." He took the coat too, since he needed it anyway, but he let Maverick pick up the snowboarding stuff. It would stay at the house so anyone could use it. "Thank you."

"Anytime." Maverick cracked up. "Can't you see Tommy doing this?"

"I can hear him now, flying straight down the mountain screaming 'Out of the way!' " He laughed himself silly. "Crikey!"

"Oh, you know it. Stark assed nekkid with his willie waving in the wind and getting icicles."

That was a picture. "Can you imagine?"

A man behind the counter coughed to get their attention.

"Oh, hi. Sorry." He gave the guy a toothy grin.

"No worries. Are you guys in town for supper? If so, try Rustico. So good, great wine. I live for the Rigatoni alla Montagna."

"Ooh. Sounds good. Thanks for the rec." Oh, there was a sale. His credit card wasn't even going to bitch at him.

"What's an 'alla Mountain'?"

"Sausage and ricotta. Spicy, meaty goodness with garlic bread."

Maverick laughed. "Fuckin' A!"

He chuckled. "Do we need a reservation?" He was joking mostly, but he couldn't wait to take Maverick there now. It was going to be epic.

"Jump on OpenTable. You'll get in. They always save a couple of spots, even if they're booked."

He did just that while Maverick paid for the amazing snowboard and looked for a reservation dinner. "You okay with seven, Mav? I don't want you to be driving home too late, you know? Or will we still be in the ER after you wipe out on that snowboard?"

"I'm waiting to use the snowboard for daylight when we're home. Seven is perfect. Sausage and cheesy pasta for the win." Maverick hauled the snowboard up, all grins. "So where next?"

"I don't know. Do you have ornaments for the tree? We can get a bunch at like Walmart or whatever, but there's a cute place here...maybe we can get a couple nice ones."

"Totally. I have some basics, you know? And some that

I've collected while I'm traveling — mostly rodeo stuff, but some that are from different cities and such."

"I love that, like a little history of where you've been on your tree. You want to put that thing in the truck before we head in?"

"I will. It's big to lug. Give me two shakes, and I'll be right back. Go browse ornaments." Mav grinned like a loon and then took off to the public parking.

He watched that pretty ass go, and then turned around to take in the mountain view again. All the snow, and the decorations. It was beautiful. He could live in a place like this. He so could.

For today he'd settle for visiting with...with his cowboy.

Sid stepped into the Christmas store, the scents of cinnamon and pine surrounding him. The entire place was lit and sparkling, and his eyes didn't know which tree to land on.

"Welcome. Merry Christmas." A soft voice came from behind one of the trees. and he stepped around, giving the sales girl a smile.

"Merry Christmas. This place is amazing."

"Just a little holiday magic. Have a look around."

"Thank you." He wandered farther into the forest of decorated trees loving how everything twinkled and sparkled. They each had a theme — Colorado, outdoor sports, forest animals, candy, nutcrackers, pink, Americana. There was even a camouflage tree.

He stopped at the forest animals because a cute little squirrel on a log caught his eye, but right next to it was a black bear, standing on its hind legs. He pulled it off the tree to look at it.

"Look at that!" Mav was at his shoulder. "That's something else, isn't it?"

He beamed, turning to give Mav a better look. "It reminded me of you. Of the house and the bears."

"I love it. I want to find a video camera one too." Maverick beamed at him. "Or one of them black and white clap deals, but a camera is better."

"One for you and one for me." He handed Mav the bear, flirting a little. "Okay. Let's look. The trees have themes. Isn't that cool?" He moved to another tree, searching for something like a camera.

"I think I need this one too. It's a cherry limeade." Maverick grinned, one side of his mouth quirking.

"Give one to Tommy for Christmas." Sid snorted.

"Oh! Good idea! He would love that. I wonder if there's anything inappropriate for Jack..."

"Naughty ornaments are on the black tree in the back," the sales girl offered from behind some other tree.

"Naughty!" He laughed and pulled Mav toward the back.

"Oh my god. Sid. I might have to get one of everything. I got lots of friends."

"Perv." He laughed, but the first thing his fingers landed on was a purple dildo ornament. "Know anyone that likes purple?"

"Oh, man. I need one of those for Jack. No, two. Then we'll send one to Hawk, and we need one to send to Sky and another for Chris..." Mav was having too much fun.

Sid just laughed, collecting purple dildo ornaments, ornaments of Santa Claus bending over with his pants down, and naked cowboy butts. "The Santa one has to go on our tree."

Our tree. Listen to him. But it was, at least this year. Hopefully longer.

"Yes. This is our first Christmas. I like that. The idea of us and first."

Damn, he had himself a cowboy poet.

He wasn't sure how they'd become a "we" all of a sudden, but it fit the pattern of his life so well he wasn't going to question it. He'd always been impulsive, taking the next good thing that came his way and jumping in with both feet. Why should this be any different? And unlike a new job, he had a lot of control over how this went. He cared about Maverick, and that connection was growing deeper every day. Today it felt like it was deeper every minute. He wanted to do this right.

"We've been a whole string of firsts for me. I like it."

"Yeah. Me too. I approve. I can't wait to give these to folks. They're going to swallow their tongues." Maverick did wicked well.

"Movie camera!" He reached out and tugged the little black old-timey movie camera off a tree. "This would work."

"Perfect! And there's a date on it." Mav took the haul to the till. "Can you wrap these up a little so I don't break them while we wander?"

"I can!" The girl grinned at them. "So, did you find everything you…needed?" Somehow she seemed too young to be making all that innuendo, but he went with it.

He laughed as she started wrapping the ornaments in tissue paper. "And a half a dozen things we absolutely did not need but had to have. Yes."

"That's the perfect answer. I told my dad that this would be a big hit. He laughed at me."

"You're a genius. Tell him I said so."

Mav paid for the haul, and she handed over a little bag with handles. "Thank you so much. Have a fun day!"

"We fully intend to. Thanks, darlin'!" Maverick headed out, all smiles.

"I seriously can't get enough of this view." His fingers

made their way right back into Mav's hand. The sun was getting lower in the sky, and he could already tell all the colors on the mountain were going to be amazing.

"I hear you. That's why I bought the house." Maverick shot him a smile. "We've got some time. Do you want a coffee? More stores?"

"A couple more stores. Then coffee. Then when we come out the sun will be going down, that's a show I need to see." And after sundown, dinner. "There's the Trading company, the T-shirt shop…"

"Want to go to the toy store? See what's there?" Oh, that was adorable.

How could he say no to that? "Come on." Sid tugged on Mav's hand. Maybe they could find a game or something fun to take home.

"Cool. I love to look at all the games and building kits and trains." Mav bounced and opened the door, the place a riot of color and light.

"Oh wow. This is like…a fancy toy store." There was wood and fabric everywhere, and not a bit of plastic in sight. They did have model kits, and also a whole wall of neat looking games. He took the handle of a wooden push duck and rolled it across the floor, watching its leather feet flap as it moved. "This is so cute."

"I have a bull one, believe it or not. Jack gave it to me for my birthday one year."

"No kidding? Jack?" He put the toy away. "He seems so…I don't know, rough? Not a toy store kind of guy." More like a kick your ass kind of guy.

"Oh, Jack has a knack for presents, weirdly enough. He can go in a place, pick up the weirdest goddamn thing on earth, and then someone will need it." Mav chuckled and shook his head. "And I think he special ordered it from a couple that are a mixture of some kinky leather worker and a wood carver."

He was sure he hadn't seen that side of Jack yet. "I have yet to not be intimidated by him. Maybe one day." He chuckled. Somehow, he doubted it.

"Yeah, he's a tough nut, but he's a good man, deep down." Maverick shrugged, and the motion wasn't embarrassed but more matter of fact. "He's not the one for me, but maybe he'll find his person someday."

"No, I'm the one for you." Sid put a little pink cowboy hat on his head and batted his eyelashes.

"You are, but I like the pink hat for me. It goes with my eyes."

"Only when you're on the good painkillers." He winked and put the hat away.

They goofed around in the toy store for a while, and he bought a neat bull rider balancing toy for the house just because he couldn't stop playing with it. Then they hit the T-shirt place where he did *not* buy the "My Heart Belongs to a Cowboy" T-shirt even though he wanted to.

Maverick stopped them on the way out of the Trading Post and pointed to the mountains. They were turning colors with the sunset and all he could do was stare. The blues he had been expecting, but the bright pinks, the orange, the shocking yellow as the sun disappeared? That was magic.

Pure magic.

Sort of like his cowboy.

He leaned back against that strong chest as the sun faded and the street lit up for the holidays. There were lights on the trees, wreaths on the lampposts and festive displays in the shop windows. "Thank you for bringing me here."

"You're welcome. I'm glad we got to see it together." Mackey kissed under his ear.

"Who knew you were such a sappy romantic?" He was only teasing, because who knew he was either?

"We'll just keep that between us, okay?" Maverick's cheek moved as he smiled.

He chuckled. "Who would I tell? No one would believe me."

"True that."

He tilted his head. "Well, Tommy might." The Australian was...weirdly empathetic where Maverick was concerned.

"You two are good friends, huh?" He pushed off Mav's chest and headed down the street toward dinner.

"Yeah. Yeah, I've known him since he was a kid. He's like my little brother. He's not quite like a son...well, I don't think so. I mean, I ain't never had a son. Or a daughter. Or a brother..."

"I think you've got plenty of brothers. They're all out there on the dirt with you every night." Family was what you made it. He had a brother, but there wasn't much between them.

"Yes. Those are my people." And Sid knew how Maverick burned to protect them.

"Where did you and Tommy meet?" The restaurant was adorable, and he moaned when Mav opened the door for him. "Smells so good."

"I was judging a bullfighting in Australia. Fun as shit. One of the guys got hooked and tossed and was out cold. Tommy hit the dirt like an arrow and saved the guy's life. I hired him that afternoon."

"Wow. Sounds like someone else I know." He gave Mav a knowing look as they were seated. "And the twins? Where did they come from again?"

"I know their momma. They're from a rodeoing family, and she knows I'll keep them safe."

"Safe?" He laughed. "There's nothing safe about bull fighting, Mav. If you wanted them safe you should have put them in concessions."

"Oh god no. Can you imagine? Those boys dealing with the *public*?"

"Oh. Well, now that you mention it..." Sid couldn't help his giggle. "Still, there have to be safe jobs."

"They're safe as houses with me. I know where they are, I don't let them drink, and I make them call home once a week." Mav winked at him, then smiled at the server. "Hey there. Give Sid here the wine list. He knows what I'll drink."

"Yes, sir."

"Wine? Fancy fancy." He opened the list and looked it over. "We'll have a half-carafe of the Chianti, please."

"Sounds good. I'll be back with bread and your wine."

He opened his menu. "Italian food, so it seemed like the right choice. What did the guy at Patagonia say we should try?"

"On the Mountain. Sausage and ricotta cheese."

"Right. Ooh."

The server put down their wine, then set out a bowl of bread and swirled some olive oil and fresh ground black pepper in a shallow bowl. "Did I overhear Rigatoni alla Montagna?"

"Yes. The guy at the sporting goods store said it was the best. I want that." Maverick wasn't the slightest bit intimidated, in fact, he was joyous, eager to experience things.

The break was doing his lover exceptionally well.

"I guess we'll have two." He chuckled. "I mean, I'm not missing out."

"Can't go wrong; it's our most popular dish. I'll bring your salads. Enjoy guys."

He watched the server head off. "He's handsome."

"Is he? He's not my type, I guess." Maverick lifted his glass. "Cheers."

"Cheers." He clinked glasses with Mav, looking right into those bright blue eyes. "You have a type? I mean, I'm probably not that type either."

"I do. I seem to be into taller fellers, and I do like a man that looks like he knows how to smile."

He smiled on cue, and then felt a little embarrassed that he had because Mav might not think it was genuine. "Smiles are sexy."

"They are." Mav winked at him. "I like yours. It suits me to the bone."

"So maybe I am your type after all." He didn't think he had a type; he'd dated all kinds of guys. But apparently his type was daredevil bullfighter. And scars. Lots of sexy scars.

"Mmhmm. You are at that, all the way." Mav reached under the table and stroked his thigh.

"You think? Me too. All the way. Isn't it strange how we ended up here? Good, but strange."

Mav seemed to ponder that. "I reckon, although rodeo time is a strange thing, you know? It don't work like normal time. What takes a few hours can change men's lives — and not just for the good or bad, and not just one."

That was true. When you lived your life in seconds, days probably seemed like forever. "That's true. And it's not that it feels wrong, it was just fast. It feels great. Right."

"Yeah. It feels like a key in a lock. I've been waiting for this for a long time."

Warmth spread from his belly, and he dropped a hand to his lap and caught Mav's fingers, squeezing them tight. "Like a key in a lock. I like the thought that I was what you've been waiting for."

"I do too." And like that was that, Maverick beamed at him, just relaxed, happy, trusting him.

"It's our own little Christmas miracle." He pointed to the air as he recognized the Eagles song. "They're even playing our song."

22

Mackey turned the Christmas music up and tossed a shitton of garland at Sid. "Where should we drape all this?"

He wanted the whole house dripping with Christmas. He'd already put a dozen inflatables up in the yard and pinned them down, along with reindeer antlers and a light up red nose on his truck.

He was in heaven.

"All along the loft." Sid's voice came from behind the pile before it landed on the couch. "And lights too, maybe?"

"Sounds like a plan. Did you see that Santa pops out of the outhouse in that one inflatable?"

"Yes! His robe is super sexy. I still like the penguins driving the tractor. I know you bought that one because I nagged you about it." Sid grabbed a long string of gold garland and headed for the loft. "I got this. You tell me if it's even."

"Will do." He stood back near the fireplace, almost tilting his head up to watch.

Sid wound the garland around the railing loosely. "Don't set your ass on fire, cowboy."

"Yeah, that sounds...actually it doesn't even sound fun." He needed to plug in the lights on the tree. It was hard to be festive with a burning butt.

Sid chuckled, smiling down at him. That smile had rarely left Sid's lips since their day in Telluride. "Does this look okay?"

"I love it. Sparkly as hell. I approve." He snapped a few pictures so he could share with Tommy and Jack.

"Excellent." Sid hurried back down the stairs looking relaxed in his new flannel and old jeans. "I'll put some lights up there too if we have enough. What next? Ornaments?"

"Yes. I found the boxes from my old house. I thought you'd like to see." They'd been carefully wrapped up every year, just like Momma had done it.

"Oh, wow. I would. This is your first Christmas here, right? So it's like, tradition and...not."

"Yep." And he loved it. He didn't care if that made him a dipshit. He had a whole life to share, and he'd decided that Sid was his.

His phone buzzed, and he picked it up. *Merry Christmas. Pretty sure the space cowboys can see your yard from Mars.*

Thanks. Wait. Wait, had he sent Jack pictures of the house yet? He didn't think so...

The doorbell rang a second later.

Sid looked up from the box he'd just opened. "Are you expecting a delivery?"

"No, and I'm not expecting company either, but I just got a text from Jack admiring the house..." He opened the door, and sure as shit, Jack stood there, looking tired and stressed as fuck.

"Ho ho ho?"

"Good lord and butter, man, get your butt in here."

"It's fucking cold out. How do you live here? That lane that passes for your driveway is covered in snow. I brought whiskey." Jack held the bottle out at arm's length.

"Good. Good. In." What the fuck had happened? He glanced at Sid, hoping to gauge his lover's thoughts.

"Uh...hey, Jack. How about a cup of coffee to warm you up?"

"I'd appreciate that." Jack froze with his coat half-off and peered around Mackey, watching Sid disappear into the kitchen. "Sid's here."

"Yep. Gonna stay too." Mackey got Jack de-coated and sat. "What happened?"

"Got into a bad wreck. I got a couple bruises, but the dude that hit my truck didn't make it. I just...It was damn nasty and I wanted to spend the holiday with family." Jack sighed, all soft. "But I hear you. You got a full house, and I'll get out of your—"

"Don't be any dumber than you have to be. I got a zillion fucking bedrooms, asshole." He was not letting Jack swing in the wind.

Jack nodded, the sigh heavier this time. Relieved. He was damn pale under his tan, the lines in his face carved deep. "Yeah. Okay. Thanks."

"I got your coffee. Come in and sit, Jack. Mav—uh, Mackey's got these great recliner seats in his couch."

Jack nodded as he moved stiffly toward the couch. "I may have fallen asleep in one a time or two."

Sid glanced at Mackey curiously as Jack got settled and then handed Jack the coffee. "Black, as I remember."

"Yessir. Thank you. Sorry I didn't call. I suppose I should have."

"Shit, you're welcome here. It's Christmas." You didn't

turn folks away at the holidays. Hell, he didn't turn folks away, at all.

Jack pointed to the tree. "Are you decorating the tree?"

Sid nodded. "Mackey found a bunch of boxes of his family's ornaments and stuff."

Jack tilted his head, and he knew what Jack was thinking, but he wondered if Sid did. "Okay. Cool."

"This is all from my house in Texas. You remember how Granny used to pull all this shit out when we'd stop in?" She loved to act like they were going to get married, have babies.

"Oh, yeah. She loved to show her things off, tell me all about how they were going to go to your kids." Jack grinned. "Give us dating advice. She was a sweet lady."

"She was." Mackey smiled, then motioned to Sid with his head. "Come help me grab the rest, honey?"

"You got it." Sid tossed Jack the remote. "In case that Mariah Carey one comes on."

That got Jack laughing as Sid followed him to get the other boxes.

"Is it okay with you if he stays? He looks like he's fixin' to tump over." He wasn't used to asking, but he reckoned he ought.

Sid gave him a confused look. "Why wouldn't it be? I mean, I hope he's going to be cool about us, but it's your house."

"I've told him about us, and it's ours — our holiday." And Mackey was praying that, one day, it would be theirs. Their house. Their home.

Sid smiled and tugged him in for a quick kiss. "There's that 'us' thing again." Sid let him go and looked around. "All of these boxes?"

"No, there's only two more. I just wanted to check in with you."

That got him a softer sort of smile. "You a good guy, you know that?" Sid picked up a box. "Thank you. Anyone who needs a place for the holidays is welcome. I hope he's okay."

"I think he will be now. Someone died. That's got to be hard." But obviously it hadn't been Jack's fault, right? Because he was here, and not wherever the wreck had been.

"Damn. Okay. Well, we can Christmas cheer him up." Sid winked and left the room with his box.

He took a deep breath. Okay, then. Sid was with him; he could handle this.

"Have you been here with all this snow before, Jack? Probably not, huh?" Sid set the box down and opened it as well.

"I haven't, no, and I appreciate y'all not kicking me to the curb. I didn't know where else to go."

"Shit, you're welcome here. You're family." And if the roles were reversed, Jack would have his back.

"This house is huge, there's room for ten more of you. Have you seen what Mav did with the downstairs guest room? It's amazing."

"Not yet. Y'all have been working hard?"

Mackey nodded and started digging through boxes. "Sid has helped me clean so much out. Our place is going to be amazing one day."

"Y'all's place?" Jack grinned at him, then glanced at Sid. "You think so, man?"

Sid's blush answered Jack's question first, but Sid glanced at him, then back at Jack. "Yeah. I hope so. I think we're giving it a go." Sid looked at him again, then pulled another ornament from the box. "I know it's...I mean, no one's more surprised than we are I think. It kind of snuck up on me."

"That's how it works, I reckon," Jack drawled. "I mean,

there's nothing wrong with finding out that y'all didn't match with folks just like you. That's exciting. I ain't worried."

He grinned at Sid, because that was as close to a blessing as they were likely to get, and it totally worked for him.

It was apparently plenty for Sid too. "Thanks, Jack. I know what that has to mean to Maverick, so it means a lot to me too. You're important to him." Sid grinned at Jack, teasing. "We'll get there."

"Yeah. By Christmas day you'll adore my happy ass. I know how to make sticky rolls."

Sid laughed. "We're going to be *great* friends."

"So Mackey, how's the—" Jack gestured to his jaw. "And everything?"

"Better. I swear, every hit takes longer to heal."

"Mhm. Everybody says the same thing. We must all be getting old." Jack squinted at him. "Will you be good for New York? Connecticut?"?"

"Shit, yes. I took out the stitches, the bruises are healing, and I'm going to be raring to go come late January." He arched one eyebrow. "Brad been on your ass about me too?"

"Buddy, Brad's aching to take you down, but none of us — not one of us — will let that happen."

Sid snorted. "He tried to get me to give him something too. He's a piece of work, huh?"

"He's a vindictive fucker, and we all know it." Jack's eyes rolled like dice, and all Mackey could do was agree.

"Well, you have a suit in your corner now, baby. It might get me fired, but I'm in your corner." Sid handed Jack an ornament. "Enough about him. Come decorate. We're spreading some cheer in here."

"Can we watch *White Christmas* while we deck the halls?" Jack asked, and Mackey snorted.

"What are you eighty? Let's watch *Die Hard*. I like the explosions."

"Those are both legit, but I vote for the…Grinch…what is that?" Sid pointed into the air. "Is that Mariah? Jack! What did you do with the remote?"

"Uh, did you give it to me?"

"Jack!" Sid laughed. "What did you do with it?"

"No Mariah, Jack. Nope." Mackey needed something less…oodley.

Sid dove for the couch and Jack shifted, coming up with it as Sid landed in his lap. "Give me that." Sid snatched it and Jack snorted as the music started to change.

"He's pretty up close," Jack murmured, and Mackey nodded.

"He is, and he's taken."

Sid's cheeks were on fire as he struggled to get up, making Mackey grin. "Sorry. Taken. Yes. You've got some guns on you though."

"I do. If you ever want a threesome…"

"Jack, be good." Mackey couldn't help his chuckle, though.

"Oh. No… no. I…" Sid chuckled. "Flattered, but Mav is enough for me."

"Oh ho! He is, huh?" Jack teased, but the tone was tickled as hell.

Sid stood, took a deep breath, and pointed at Jack. "Stop that."

Jack stared for a second, then burst out laughing, which got him going, and Sid was soon to follow.

"You two. This tree-trimming party needs boozy coffee." Sid picked up Jack's empty mug and headed for the kitchen.

Jack hauled himself out of his recliner with a groan. "He's cute…"

"He's hot as hell, and I think I'm stupid for him."

"You must be, you're letting him call you Maverick." Jack made a half-hearted attempt to hang a ball on the tree. "I'm happy for you. Even if he is a Yankee."

"Nobody's perfect, man." He winked at Jack, tickled. "I talked to him. He's more than willing to have you here too."

"He better be. Me, Tommy, the twins...we're part of the package." Jack winked. "But it's good of him. This was shaping up to be a tough one."

"Yeah. Good thing I ain't mailed your Christmas yet." He winked at Jack, then sobered. "You okay, buddy?"

Jack nodded. "I'm fine. I was trying to feel sorry for myself after that accident, but you're not going to allow that, right? So, I guess I'm trimming a goddamn Christmas tree."

"You are. You are trimming a goddamn tree and singing goddamn carols and eating goddamn cookies." He fought his smile with all he had.

"And drinking goddamn boozy coffee!" Sid appeared with three mugs of something that looked like coffee, smelled like whiskey and was covered in whipped cream.

"Ooh...whipped cream!" He was all over adult beverages.

"We're putting on *White Christmas* because the old man asked for it." Sid handed out drinks and picked up the magical remote that turned off the music and turned on the TV. He got that system when he bought the couch with the recliners. It had been a good purchase.

"Old man?" Jack looked offended until he took a taste of his drink and then he grinned like a kid in a candy store. "Ooh. That's good stuff."

Mackey offered Sid a smile and a kiss, loving the freedom to do it — to take a hard kiss in front of friends. Sid squeaked in surprise, but quickly melted right into him.

"Down in front!" Jack waved them out of them way. "Move over you two. I can't see Bing."

Sid grinned against his lips but didn't move. "Turn on the tree lights? I think it's easier to decorate that way."

"Lord save me from new relationship energy," Jack rumbled as he headed to turn on the lights.

"Did the safety man really just say 'new relationship energy'?" Sid's grin was wicked.

"Uh-huh." Mackey didn't even know what that meant, exactly, but it had been said.

The tree lights came on, making the living room even merrier than it already was.

"Ooh." Sid turned around to see the tree, leaning back against him. "Now it feels like Christmas."

"Yessir. It's just right." It was, and he was going to give thanks for it. Santa had been good to him.

23

Merry Christmas, Dad.

Eight a.m. Colorado time was ten o'clock Pennsylvania time, so Sid knew Dad was up, probably having breakfast with Lance and the kids. He didn't really expect a response, but he wasn't going to be the one who closed that door either, so he left that text out there for a bit before giving up and putting his phone down.

There was more snow out in Maverick's back yard than he had seen in one place in his entire life. It had started Christmas Eve morning, and it didn't show any signs of letting up any time soon. It was a pristine sea of white—no footprints, no tire tracks, no sign of life anywhere out there.

There was plenty of life in here though, and he decided to go crawl back in bed with it.

Mav was curled up in the big bed, snuggled into the sheets. He was so cute, his butt up in the air. He loved how relaxed Mav was now, how well his lover slept in this house, with him.

And he was pretty happy about a naked cowboy in his bed too. That butt was calling to him so ditched his robe as he climbed back into bed, got a good handful of ass, and gave it a squeeze.

Maverick arched and rocked a second, then stretched, showing off all that fine body, all the muscles and scars.

"Merry Christmas, handsome." Sid snuggled in, stretching out alongside Mav, stealing warmth from all of that skin.

"Merry Christmas, lover. How's you this fine morning?" Maverick tugged him close.

"It is a fine morning. I was just checking out the snow. There's a lot of it. Like, a lot. I hope you either have a plow or know a guy." Sid chuckled. "Or we'll be here until July."

"I do not have a plow, but that might be a blast. I got a John Deere in the barn. I could totally get a plow attachment." Mav blinked over at him, eye lines going deep as he grinned. "How fun would that be?"

"Your idea of fun is a little suspect." Mav probably would love it, though. "I would have a great time drinking cocoa in my fuzzy slippers and watching you drive around in the cold."

"I could make huge snow things with a plow, though. Snow piles up to your ears." Life sized snow people. Great. Just what Maverick needed.

"The ones the big plows make in parking lots are three times taller than my ears." He regretted saying that as soon as it was out of his mouth. "Not that you want a huge plow like that. You have grass to consider."

"Yes, and I need to attach it to my tractor." Maverick wasn't joking.

"Hey, baby? Why don't you hire someone to plow us out so you can spend more time in bed with me?" Surely that would work.

"Oh now, that's good to hear. I do love a man with a great idea."

Bingo. He scritched his fingers through the hair on Mav's fuzzy chest. "What are your Christmas traditions? I never even asked."

"Mmm...about the same as everybody else, I guess. We open presents and relax for the rest of the day, watch some football. I got a roast for supper."

"We didn't go shopping for each other, so your present is going to have to be me. And I'm already unwrapped."

"Mmhmm...we got the new TV for up here and a new router. That's a good present." Maverick dragged one callused hand over his ass.

He leaned into the touch. "It is. And the snow. I can't believe it's Christmas already."

"I know. This has been the best break, honey. I have loved every second, and given the way it started, I was expecting a shitshow." Maverick touched his newest scar. "A lonely one."

"I don't know what I was expecting. I knew I wasn't going back east, so it was easy to volunteer to drive, you know? But I literally had no plan for after we got here. This...I never thought this..." Honestly, he'd been expecting a lonely one too.

"No, me either, but you know...I'm not going to deny you a bit. I'm loving getting to know you, to be with you."

"You're definitely making my Christmas merry." And they'd decked the place out with Jack's help. The place was covered in lights and garland and the tree was amazing.

They had cookies, a cheese and meat tray for lunch, and a huge roast for supper. There were a smattering of presents under the tree, and snow. All that snow.

He grinned wickedly. "Should we dress Jack up as Santa?"

"Oh, that would be a hoot. I know he's got a set of bright red longies."

He laughed. "Maybe if we get him drunk enough..." Sid admired Mav's easy smile, the way it lit up his lover's bright blue eyes. He loved this lazy holiday morning vibe. "We don't have to get up yet, do we?"

"No. Santa has come and gone, and I am perfectly happy, right here." Maverick pulled him close for a kiss, wrapping him in tight.

Mav's kiss made his skin tingle and his balls heavy. Yeah, that was a Christmas memory he could get into. He arched into his cowboy, one hand sliding down Mav's back to his ass and holding on.

"Mmm..." That earned him a warm, happy smile, and then Mav rolled over, bringing him on top.

"All right. I get to be the rodeo cowboy." He straddled Mav's hips, pushing up with his hands on his cowboy's chest. He rolled the little pink nubs there with his thumbs grinning down at his lover.

Mav's teeth sank into his bottom lip as Sid teased. He liked that, how Maverick showed him how good everything felt. He dropped down again, going after those sensitive spots with his mouth, licking and sucking each in turn.

"Jesus, honey." Mav's eyes crossed, and he bucked for Sid, enough to feel that heavy cock starting to fill.

"Not Jesus." He bit one nipple, suddenly but gently.

"R-right." Mav's fingers tangled in his hair, cupping his head. "Damn, honey."

He couldn't help laughing softly.

"I know. I do. You make me dizzy as hell." Mav drew him up into a hard, happy kiss. "I'm so damn happy."

Nobody watching Maverick on the arena floor would think he was this sweet and capable of this much joy off the dirt. Even Sid thought at first that he was a bit of an ass. "Not happy enough yet." He slid away, moving down Mav's body toward that perfect prick. "Soon though."

"Soon." Mav panted for him, lips parted, eyes so focused. "Jesus, I need you bad. You're so fucking pretty."

"You smell so good. This perfect prick—" He licked it, bathing the head and savoring the salty taste.

Mav's head fell back against the pillows, a deep, raw sound tearing from his chest. Sid let that beautiful sound spur him on as he tasted every bit of skin down the shaft, around heavy balls that twitched at his touch and back up again, determined to test Mav's patience and drive him wild.

Mav pushed up on his elbows, eyes burning down at him, lips parted and hungry. He only held Mav's eyes for a second, but it was long enough to make his own cock take notice, and he moaned and swallowed the gorgeous cock down, working it with purpose.

"Oh, fuck. You got a mouth like a dream." Mav's voice was rough as a cob, and one leg drew up, sliding against his cheek.

He was all about that voice. He pulled up and drove his tongue through the cleft in the swollen head again and again, knowing how to drive his cowboy out of his mind.

Mav began to buck, feeding his soul with those desperate little noises, the wild need. He hummed, palming Mav's balls, then swallowed hard. Like he'd demanded it, Mav shot for him, coming like there was no tomorrow.

Ho Ho Ho. Sid sucked and swallowed and licked, keeping Mav flying as long as he could. Fuck, that was so gratifying, the way Mav just let go with him—his big, strong bull fighter was truly putty in his hands sometimes. It was a secret he was happy to keep just between them.

Maverick slumped back in the bed, hands opening and closing in the sheets convulsively. He let up finally, nuzzling and slowly kissing his way back up Maverick's incredible body, inspecting muscles and scars with his fingers as he went. "So beautiful."

"Thank you. Damn, love. Merry Christmas to me."

"Mhm." He kissed his cowboy, softly, slowly. "The best part of that gift is there's more of it. Any time you want."

"Oh, honey." Maverick stared into him, straight into his soul. "I want. I want it all. Forever."

"Yes," he said simply. Whatever that meant, however they made that happen, he was in. "All of it, forever."

"Then I got all I need." Maverick pulled him down, kissing him good and hard, making all the promises he might need.

For this morning, and his mornings going forward.

24

Mackey watched Jack pace — up the stairs, down the stairs, to the back kitchen door, to the big bay windows, back up. It was dizzying, and he supposed he would be worried if he didn't know Jack, inside and out.

Someone was fixin' to hit the road.

The next round, Mackey stood and got in Jack's way. "Babe, if you have to go, go."

Jack flushed, looking more than a little hangdog. "I just... you know me, Mackey."

"I do." And the fact that Jack always ran was one of a thousand reasons they were just friends with benefits. Had been, he guessed. Mackey needed someone that loved him, wanted to share his life and his home. He didn't blame Jack one bit. A man was built like the good Lord intended him to be. No one could argue that.

"This has been good though. I appreciate you letting me crash Christmas with your...with Sid." Jack rolled his shoulders and took a step back, putting a little more space between them.

"It's serious, you know. Like I'm talking forever. It's what

I need." And he prayed every day that Jack got that too — forever.

Jack shook his head. "That's good, Mackey. That's a good thing for you. He's serious also. I can see it in the way he looks at you. You're lucky."

"I am." And he wasn't going to say he was sorry, because he wasn't. But he hated this for Jack. Hated it.

"I know." Jack winked at him, and Mackey wasn't sure what that all meant, but it didn't matter.

What mattered was that Jack was hurting, and there wasn't a thing he could do about it.

"So, I'll see you soon in the arena, right?" Jack ducked into the guest room and came back with his bag, already packed. He must have gotten up early. He hiked it up on his shoulder. "Can't wait to hear what the twins got up to."

"Trouble. The answer is always trouble, man." He shook his head and grinned. "I'll see you in three weeks."

"You will do." Jack led him to the door and offered a hand to shake. "Happy New Year."

Oh, he didn't think so. He marched up to Jack and hugged him, hard. "Happy New Year, man. I'll see you soon. Be careful driving."

The hug he got in return was just as hard, and if it lasted just a second too long, well, that was because he was Jack. He'd always be Jack. "Always." Jack gave him a nod and headed out, waving before he got into his truck.

He locked the door and went to stoke the fire. Lord have mercy.

"I put the champagne in the fridge to chill." Sid came from the kitchen and headed his way, wearing a stack of sparkly cardboard top hats on his head. He blew a little noisemaker horn, and it echoed in the open room. "It's going to be a good year."

"It is. It's going to be the best." He stood up and went to Sid, seeking a hug. "Jack headed out, honey."

"What? I brought him a hat. I didn't know he had New Year's plans." Sid actually looked a little disappointed. How cute was that?

"I don't know, honey. He was...he wanted to move on. That's how he is. He comes and goes."

"Danny said that about him. Danny said a lot about him." Sid grinned, then set the hats down on the coffee table. "I was worried he'd be...I don't know. Weird. Jealous? Something."

"He's Jack. We wanted to be more than friends, but I want forever, he wants everyone."

"Well, then you're both getting what you want. Right?" Sid leaned in for a kiss, and he pushed right up into it. He was feeling — he wasn't sure what it was, but he knew Sid was the one that could fix it.

"Mm." Sid searched his eyes as the kiss ended. "What's the matter?"

"I hate that he's lonely. I hope he finds what I did. Someone to turn him inside out." It just wasn't going to be him.

"He will, if that's what he's after. He seems like the kind of man that knows how to get what he wants." Sid drew a finger down his chest. "And don't you feel guilty because you have it."

"No. No, I feel grateful that I have you. You are the man I've looked for my whole life." Mackey knew it, and the words filled him with faith.

"You say the most...romantic things." Sid squeezed his fingers. "When you speak from your heart like that."

"I'm telling the truth." Sid's words made him beam, though, his happiness pouring through him.

"I know. And you have to know you're everything to me, Mav. You're my family now. You're my home. This is my home."

"Yes." All he could do was offer Sid a kiss, thanking his lover with all he was.

Sid took the kiss and stayed close, arms around his waist. "So, we're a party of two for New Year's Eve?"

"We are. I think that's perfect — you, me, champagne, dancing." It wasn't a fancy party, but it was one where he could kiss Sid at midnight.

"Dinner. Countdown party on TV." Sid turned him in a circle. "You've become a good dancer too. That's what practice gets you."

"You've helped me learn to like it." And it was helpful, to have time off.

"Yeah?" Sid picked up the remote and music filled the room. "Maybe you should lead this time."

"I can do that. I got your back." And Sid's front too, for that matter. He sent a little prayer up for Jack's safety and happiness, then he let it go.

His dance card was full.

❄

Sid fixed two cups of coffee and took them upstairs. It was his last night in Colorado, at least for the foreseeable future, and he'd made a date with his man to watch the sky change as the sun went down.

He ducked into the bathroom and set one mug on the counter for Maverick who was in the shower. "Almost sunset, baby. I'll be on the balcony."

"Mhm."

They'd worked their asses off the last few days. They

finished the demolition on the master bathroom, taking it down to the studs so it was ready for renovation, and they'd taken down a wall that was dividing what Mav wanted to be one big master bedroom. Today they'd cleaned up, hauling everything out to the dumpsters.

He was exhausted. Good exhausted; they'd made it fun, but his body was tired. Mav was strong and could be hard to keep up with.

Sid pulled on a hoodie, took his coffee out through the bedroom doors to the balcony and looked out over the darkening trees, but he really had eyes on the sky. He loved all the colors. If he had to pick one thing he was going to miss about this house, it was the sky.

He wanted to believe that he and Maverick would be back here together when it snowed. He was choosing to. But things didn't always work out as planned and a little voice in his head worried about what was going to happen once they were back on the road.

They had positions, politics, closets and... Still, Mav never flinched at the idea of forever. It's what Sid wanted too, so he'd go after it like that was the plan.

He sipped his coffee and watched as the sky started turning colors, willing Maverick to hurry it up. He wanted company. He wanted his cowboy.

"Hey, pretty. Did I make it in time?" Maverick looked exhausted and happy, just like him.

"Yeah, look. It's just starting. I was just wishing you were here." Sid took Maverick's hand and pulled him closer. "Last one for a while."

"Yeah, but next time we come home, we'll have a master suite." Maverick was so generous with that *we*.

"We will. And it will be amazing. And all your cowboy friends can stay downstairs." He supposed if this really worked out, he'd give up his place in New York. That thought scared him a little, made him nervous. But it wouldn't make sense to float the place.

"Yes. Yes, that's what all the bedrooms downstairs will be for." Maverick took his hand. "This is starting to feel more like home, huh?"

He nodded. It was. More than anywhere he'd been since he struck out on his own. "It is. Not just the bedroom but… the view, the land. The mountains. They feel like ours."

"Yeah." The sun began to sink, and they watched the skies turn pink and then bright orange.

"Thanks for this, Mav. You ready to get back to work?"

"I am. It's about time. The cowboys need protecting, and for the whole world to look at 'em."

"Cool. I'm ready too. It'll make me appreciate this more." Sid gave his lover a wink. "Are you going to let me drive?"

"I am. I'm going to rest and mess with your head the whole way."

He snorted. "Oh good. I'm really looking forward to that."

25

"Boys! You get your asses moving!" The twins had gotten slow over Christmas, the fudge and the beer and the long break making them sluggish.

Mackey would fix that shit.

"We're moving!" Grainger shouted back.

Hayden gave his brother a shove. "I'm moving. You're like one of those…slow, tree hugging things."

"A sloth, idiot."

"See? You even know what it's called!"

"Shut up."

"Catch me!" Hayden took off, but it wasn't too long before Grainger caught up.

"Oi, you want I should kill them?"

"Nah, Tommy." Mackey didn't even try to hide his smile. "Someone would notice. Cameras and shit, you know?"

He nodded toward his Sid, who was growling about some technical shit.

"Roigh. Cameras." Tommy nodded and grinned, white teeth standing out against tanned skin. Someone had gotten some sun over the break. "Can't trust 'em."

"Can't trust the suits who use them against us, that's the truth."

"That's a sexy scar you got there, Mother, but it looks like you're all good. Ready to get back in there?"

"You know it. I'm ready to show these bulls who's boss." Ready to learn about traveling with Sid, ready to hear no end of shit about dating a Yankee that wore a sports coat.

Ready to sleep with his man every night, even if it was in a lot of different beds.

"I can't believe you've left me on my own with those hooligans." Tommy rolled his eyes. "I mean...who the hell do I have to sleep with to get my own room, man? Oh. Wait. I guess you answered that one." Tommy's grin was wide as his face, teeth glinting at him.

"Shut up, asshole." He couldn't stop smiling though, and when Sid glanced at him, he got a raised eyebrow, a slow smile. "Go on, now. Chase the puppies and make them do tricks for us."

"Kinky, Mother. Kink. Ky."

"That's me. The master of pervyosity. Now, cowboy up or go get in the truck. We got a show to do."

And afterward, he'd have Sid.

Over and over, God willing and the creek didn't rise.

Interested in learning more about BA's cowboys and Jodi's gentlemen? Want free fiction and news? Join our newsletters!

What's Up with Jodi
https://readerlinks.com/l/2317334

Spurs and Shifters
https://lp.constantcontact.com/su/A9CRUzp/baandjulia

WINDOW DRESSING
Jodi Payne and BA Tortuga

When bull rider Sterling Kingsolver wins a national rodeo championship in a stunning upset, he becomes the public face of the rodeo league. But the big bosses had other plans, and Sterling knows he's in trouble. Worst of all, though, he's headed to New York City to do a publicity junket. Sterling is a quiet cowboy from New Mexico, and all the fancy trappings of his new title don't sit so well with him.

Jonas Burke is an experienced public relations assistant. He's been hired by the rodeo league to get a hick cowboy from the middle of nowhere cleaned up and presentable by New York standards, and he's been told to cancel his week-long Christmas vacation to do it.

The two men square off a couple of times, but as they get to know each other, Jonas begins to understand what makes a real cowboy tick, and Sterling starts to realize there's more to Jonas than a flashy smile. While taking in the sparkle and joy that is Christmas in New York City, their friendship slowly becomes more. But when trouble catches up with them, Sterling's days in the city come to an end and Jonas nearly loses his job. Facing that infamous midnight hour, Sterling and Jonas have to decide what their New Year will bring.

Window Dressing is an opposites attract, enemies to lovers romance featuring a rodeo cowboy, a city boy in a suit, and the magic of New York City at the holidays.

Read More Here

Happy Holidays, Y'all!

We want to thank you for giving Cowboy Protection a try. We hope you enjoyed the story.

If you can spare a few minutes to post a review at the retail website where you made your purchase, we'd very much appreciate it!

Don't forget to "like" our Facebook pages and groups to keep up with all the news--new releases, sales announcements, giveaways, sneak peeks-- and of course the rodeo pictures, coffee memes and just general fun. We'd love to have all y'all!

Yeehaw and thanks for reading!

BA & Jodi

ABOUT JODI

JODI takes herself way too seriously and has been known to randomly break out in song. Her men are imperfect but genuine, stubborn but likable, often kinky, and frequently their own worst enemies. They are characters you can't help but fall in love with while they stumble along the path to their happily ever after. For those looking to get on her good side, Jodi's addictions include nonfat lattes, Malbec and tequila any way you pour it.

Website: jodipayne.net
Newsletter: https://readerlinks.com/l/2317334
All Jodi's Social Links: linktr.ee/jodipayne

ABOUT BA

Texan to the bone and an unrepentant Daddy's Girl, BA Tortuga spends her days with her basset hounds, getting tattooed, texting her grandbabies, and eating Mexican food. When she's not doing that, she's writing. She spends her days off watching rodeo, knitting and surfing Pinterest in the name of research. BA's personal saviors include her wife, Julia Talbot, her best friends, and coffee. Lots of coffee. Really good coffee.

Having written everything from fist-fighting rednecks to hard-core cowboys to werewolves, BA does her damnedest to tell the stories of her heart, which was raised in Northeast Texas, but has heard the call of the high desert and lives in the Sandias. With books ranging from hard-hitting GLBT romance, to fiery ménages, to the most traditional of love stories, BA refuses to be pigeon-holed by anyone but the voices in her head.

BA loves to talk to her readers and can be found at http://batortuga.com/ and her newsletter signup link is http://bit.ly/BAJulianews

AVAILABLE FROM JODI & BA

The Cowboy and the Dom Trilogy

First Rodeo, Book One

Razor's Edge, Book Two

No Ghosts, Book Three

The Soldier and the Angel, a Cowboy and Dom Novel

Sin Deep, a Cowboy and Dom Novel

East Meets Westerns

(single titles)

Wrecked

Flying Blind

Special Delivery, A Wrecked Holiday Novel

Temptation Ranch

Window Dressing

Cowboy Protection

The Higher Elevation Series

Heart of a Cowboy

Land of Enchantment

Keeping Promises

Bigger Than Us

The Triskelion Series

Breaking the Rules

Making a Mark

Making the Rules

Les's Bar Series

Just Dex

Hide Bound

The Lone Star Series

Tending Tyler

Roped In

The Collaborations Series

Refraction

Syncopation

Puzzles Series

Cryptic